WINTER'S AWAKENING

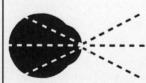

This Large Print Book carries the
Seal of Approval of N.A.V.H.

WINTER'S AWAKENING

SHELLEY SHEPARD GRAY

THORNDIKE PRESS
A part of Gale, Cengage Learning

GALE
CENGAGE Learning™

Detroit • New York • San Francisco • New Haven, Conn • Waterville, Maine • London

GALE
CENGAGE Learning™

Thorndike Press® Large Print Christian Romance.
The text of this Large Print edition is unabridged.
Other aspects of the book may vary from the original edition.
Set in 16 pt. Plantin.

LIBRARY OF CONGRESS CATALOGING-IN-PUBLICATION DATA

Gray, Shelley Shepard.
  Winter's awakening / by Shelley Shepard Gray.
    p. cm. — (Thorndike Press large print Christian romance)
  ISBN-13: 978-1-4104-2780-9
  ISBN-10: 1-4104-2780-3
  1. Amish—Fiction. 2. Large type books. I. Title.
PS3607.R3966W365 2010b
813'.6—dc22   2010009708

Published in 2010 by arrangement with Avon Inspire, an imprint of HarperCollins Publishers.

This book is dedicated to Lesley.
You've taught me so much . . .
so many things only a daughter
can teach a mom.
I'm so grateful for you,
and so proud of the young lady
you've become.

PROLOGUE

"The weather's getting a fair sight colder, wouldn't you say?" Gretta Hershberger asked Joshua as they rode along the black-topped winding roads just south of Sugar-creek. A new dampness clung to the breeze and stung her cheeks, making her glad they were sitting right next to each other in his courting buggy.

"It is," Joshua replied after a moment.

It wasn't much of a reply to Gretta's way of thinking. No, his answer had sounded more like a grunt under his breath.

She eyed him a little more closely under her black bonnet, hoping against hope that she'd discover some clue to help her understand what was going on with Joshua. But unfortunately — or fortunately, perhaps — he looked the same as he always did.

Joshua was a handsome one, and that was the truth. At almost twenty years of age, he'd long since lost any awkwardness of his

7

teenaged years. When he was standing, he towered over her by a good six or seven inches. And his thick blond hair and finely honed cheekbones had always been attractive.

So had his eyes. Joshua had the most wondrous grayish green eyes that more than a few people in their community said reminded them of the ocean.

For years, Gretta had always thought he was a most attractive boy. Lately, she'd been pleased to think of him as her sweetheart. Though he'd held her heart since the first time he took her skating, over the last year he'd become increasingly more ardent. Now he took her for buggy rides almost every week. Today, though, he was behaving mighty churlishly. "Um, have you heard if snow is in the forecast?" she asked, anxious for any type of conversation.

"No."

She shifted a bit, thankful for the thick quilt covering their legs. And, because Joshua was not looking in her direction, nor offering her much conversation, she looked around.

Oh, but Sugarcreek was a pretty place to call home. Here and there, farmhouses mixed with lovely buildings that English architects had fashioned into Swiss styles.

The tourists said some of the buildings looked like Swiss chalets.

In the distance, a trio of dairy cows walked along the fence line, as if they were looking for friends. And when they passed Caleb Yoder's farm, she saw several of his *kinner* out with a new batch of kittens. "Oh, Joshua, did you see those kittens? Black as night, they were."

He looked to his right, beyond her to the Yoder farm. Gretta knew the moment he spied the kittens because his mouth curved into a reluctant smile. "It looks to be a big litter, *jah?* How many did you count?"

"Four, I think. Maybe more."

He chuckled. "Caleb will be wanting to sell some cats sometime soon, wouldn't you say?"

"I suppose."

Pulling on the reins, he stopped the buggy at a stop sign, then, after a pair of automobiles passed them, he guided his horse onto her street.

Gretta was surprised. They'd not been out for even an hour. "Are you taking me home already?"

"*Jah.* I think it's time."

"Why?" Almost teasing, she turned to him. "Did I say something to upset you?"

Joshua looked uncomfortable. "I just don't

feel like riding in the buggy this evening."

"But why not?"

His eyes flashed. "Why do you do that, Gretta? Why do you question everything so much?"

Well now, that stung. "Everything? Joshua, all I asked was why you didn't want to ride for a while longer."

As his horse Jim guided them along her quiet rural street, Joshua answered. "Truth is, I am upset with something."

"What?"

"A group of our friends came into the store today when I was working. They were full of mischief about us."

"I don't understand."

His voice hardened. "They said they heard you speaking to Miriam about your plans for us after church last Sunday. You were talking about where you wanted to live . . . how many *bopplis* we might have. As if something had been decided between us."

Gretta's face flushed. Yes, she had been talking childishly with her best friend. They'd been imagining living near each other one day. Before long, their talk had turned to what their lives would be like after they were both married and had a houseful of babies. Giggling, they'd even chatted about homes and such. Gretta had even told

10

Miriam all about the dishes she'd recently purchased for her hope chest.

Of course, she'd never imagined the conversation would be repeated. "I . . . I didn't realize anyone but Miriam heard me."

"Well, they did. And once more, you shouldn't have been saying such things at all."

"But we've been courting —"

"Nothing's been decided, Gretta. Your talk embarrassed me something awful."

"I'm sorry," she murmured. And she was. In the future, she'd make sure she didn't share silly dreams in a crowded place. "You are right. I shouldn't have said anything."

"I haven't even joined the church, you know," he added, as if her apology meant nothing to him. "And I don't know if I'm ready to grow my beard neither."

Since most Amish men waited to grow their beards until they exchanged wedding vows, Gretta frowned. "I thought you were going to get baptized soon. After all, I joined the church last year."

"That was your choice. I'm not ready. I'll not be pushed."

"I won't push. But —"

"Gretta, stop being such a *blabbermaul,* would you? Can we just stop talking for a while?"

11

Afraid to say a word, she nodded. But a terrible sense of foreboding filled her as she sat by his side. *They were fighting.* And, even worse, they were doing what her parents did after their arguments — retreating into a cold, frosty silence.

A lump formed in her throat as she recalled the many tension-filled evenings spent in her home. Nights filled with a simmering anger that she and her sister tried not to speak of but could never escape.

And now here she was, in the same situation with Joshua. But it wasn't supposed to be like this. She'd been sure he was the one for her. That she was the right *frau* for him. But now, as the silence continued, Gretta felt a true sense of foreboding flow through her, breaking her heart just a bit.

No, this wasn't right at all.

Finally, Joshua brought Jim to a stop in the front of her house. Her parents had bought the two-story white clapboard house from an elderly English couple shortly before her sister Beth had been born. After disabling the electricity and pulling out all the carpet, it had become home. Yes, it was pretty as a picture on the outside. Inside, though, things were far less welcoming.

Remembering Joshua's harsh words, Gretta quickly pushed aside the quilt covering her legs and climbed down. As soon as her boots touched the pavement, she straightened her cape and escaped to her home's front walkway. She didn't bother to say anything to Joshua. After all, hadn't he asked for her silence?

"Gretta, wait."

Turning, she eyed him warily.

Looking sheepish, he hopped out of the buggy. "Listen, I'm sorry. I've been worrying about a number of things, and I took those worries out on you. I shouldn't have snapped at you like that."

"I wish you wouldn't have, too, Joshua," she said. "But you mustn't take back your words. I think you meant them. I think you were truly angry that I was talking about us, like we had a future planned."

Looking pained, he stepped closer. "Well, yes, I was upset about the teasing, but I didn't mean everything I said. I promise I didn't. Please, let's just forget about it all."

"I'll do my best," she replied with a forced smile. When he tipped his hat and got back in the buggy, she turned and walked to the front door. But as she entered her home, Gretta knew she'd just spoken a lie.

She wasn't about to forget any of the things he said. Just as importantly, she wasn't about to forget how she'd felt, sitting

13

by his side in silence. She'd felt trapped and lonely and worried.

Just like she felt at home when her parents argued.

With a feeling of despair, Gretta realized . . . if this was her future with Joshua, she didn't want it. Not even if she loved him with all her being.

Never again did she want to enter a house and hear only silence. She wanted her marriage to be one of peace and happiness. If Joshua Graber couldn't give her that, perhaps they weren't suited to each other after all.

But oh, how that would break her heart.

CHAPTER 1

"Whatcha think they're doin' now?" Anson asked, swinging his scuffed black boots against the thick wood planks of the fence that divided their farm from that of the new neighbors.

Joshua Graber pulled his attention away from the two teenagers he could almost see on the other side of the thick brush of woods. "I don't know."

"Come on. Sure ya do. Didn't you say they got an automobile?"

"They're *English*. 'Course they got an automobile. And it's called a *truck*. You should know that."

"It ain't my fault that I can't see over and through all those trees. I'm not as tall as you."

Joshua shook his head in a futile effort to curb his impatience with his nine-year-old brother. "Believe me, I know that. You're too young to be much use to anyone."

15

"Mamm says I'm mighty helpful. And I am." Swinging his legs hard for emphasis, Anson almost lost his balance. *Again.* Josh held out an arm to catch a fall even as he grumbled to himself. This *bruder* needed a keeper for day and night.

Time and again, Anson was always doing things without thinking and coming to trouble. Joshua couldn't remember if he'd been that awkward and clumsy at nine. Being that age felt like a lifetime ago.

Most likely 'cause it was. Now he worked full-time at his family's store and helped out around the farm whenever he could. It was only because he was preparing to take Gretta out later for a buggy ride that he was home.

When Anson fidgeted again, Joshua placed a hand on his brother's bony shoulders. "Careful, now."

As expected, his little brother shrugged off his touch. "Stop babyin' me. I won't fall."

"Oh, settle down, Anson," their sister Judith said as she approached. "No one wants to spend the day at the hospital patching up a broken bone."

Anson spread his legs a little wider, obviously hoping to get as firmly situated as possible. "I haven't broken a *gnocha* in two years."

"We're probably due, then, I reckon," Joshua said.

"Don't call on trouble," Judith warned. At seventeen, Judith, too, had long since left behind her childhood. Since leaving school after the eighth grade, she divided her time between helping out with their younger brothers and sisters and working at the store.

But though she was mature, Judith wasn't too old to care about the new family living on the other side of the property line. "What are they doing now? What can ya see?"

"Nothing," Josh replied. "The older boy's truck is black and shiny — he looks to have just wiped off a bunch of salt from the roads. Next to him is a boy in between Anson and Caleb's age — about eleven or so. He just cleared off some snow from their driveway. They've got a boom box out, but I don't think they're playing any music."

"What's a boom box?" Anson asked, his voice as high and whiny as ever.

"It's a thing that plays music, but you can carry it around," Judith answered.

"Why would you need such a thing?"

Before Josh could tell Anson to stop asking so many questions, Judith answered

17

again. "So you can hear music and sing along."

"When are we ever going to meet them? I want to meet our new neighbors."

"Daed said we should give them some time," Joshua said, trying to act as if he could care less. "Remember, they only moved in three days ago."

Fidgeting again, Anson said, "You think they'll be like the Wilsons? I liked them."

Their old neighbors had been good folk. Though English, they had much in common with their Amish neighbors. They'd even invited the whole Graber family to their daughter's wedding last summer. "I don't know."

"Wonder where they came from." After a pause, Anson asked, "Do you reckon they'll be from Milwaukee?"

Judith chuckled. "Just because the Wilsons moved to Milwaukee doesn't mean that the new neighbors come from there. The English live everywhere, and move a lot."

"Not like us."

"That is true. Most English are not like us. We're here to stay in Sugarcreek." Joshua was about to expand on that when he spied a new member of the family appear on their driveway. She had short curly hair and wore

18

a red sweater, some kind of fuzzy brown jacket, mittens, and jeans. He could hardly look away. Oh, but she sure was pretty.

"What do you see now?" Judith asked.

"What? Oh, nothing."

She hopped up on the bottom rung of their fence. "I see three people there, but a branch is blocking my view. Who just joined them?"

He swallowed. "No one. Just a girl."

Judith brightened. "How old?"

"I don't know. Maybe seventeen or eighteen." It was hard to tell. The girl across the thicket of trees looked to be Judith's height, but their clothes were so different, it was hard to tell.

Eagerness filled his sister's eyes. "Wouldn't it be wonderful-*gut* to have some neighbors our age? Maybe she and I could become friends."

"Maybe. Maybe not." The English girl looked a fair bit different than Judith in her gray dress, black apron, and black sturdy boots.

"What do ya mean by that?" Anson asked.

"Nothing. She just looks different. That's all."

"I wanna see! Lift me up on your shoulders."

"You're too big for that."

"Well, I'm too short to see anything from here. I'm never the right size." With a frown, Anson squirmed on the snowy fence — even going so far as to try to balance on his knees.

"Careful, you're gonna fall," Judith warned.

"I won't. I won't! You just don't wanna let me see. You want to keep our new neighbors all to yourself."

Josh turned to Judith and raised a brow. "That's right. I want to keep our new neighbors — whom I've never met — all to myself."

Sharing a look of amusement, Judith joined in. "You should stop being so *veesht,* so mean, Joshua."

Anson rocked again. "I wanna —"

Too late, Joshua held out a hand to him. As if in slow motion, their little brother bypassed his grip and fell backward onto the hard ground — frozen from their most recent cold spell. Smack on his left arm.

After a brief momentous pause, a cry rang out loud enough for everyone miles around to hear.

Joshua was vaguely aware of a number of exclamations around them. Of his father running toward them along the narrow gravel path that that Caleb was to have already shoveled clear of snow . . .

20

Judith knelt and looked at Anson's arm with concern. "I fear it's broken," she said to their father over his cries. "There now, Anson," she murmured, as she leaned closer and wrapped one of her arms around his back. "We'll help you, I promise."

Joshua stood up as his father took over, fussing over Anson, and then gingerly picking him up into his strong arms. Josh was just about to follow when he spied the three figures they'd been watching peering at the lot of them with curiosity.

Just a mere few yards away.

He nodded a greeting. When they didn't say a word, he felt obligated to speak. "My *bruder* . . . I mean, um, my brother fell. I think he broke his arm."

The oldest still stared — his expression openly rude. Josh glared right back.

But the youngest boy didn't look to be nearly as standoffish. Stepping a little closer, he reached out to touch the brim of Josh's black hat. "Why are you dressed like that?"

"Ty, don't touch," the girl said. Looking Josh's way, she murmured, "I'm sorry."

Josh waved her off. It was easier to face the boy and the questions than his confusing feelings about the girl — she was even prettier close up. "I dress like this because I'm Amish."

21

"But why a black hat? Why don't —"

"Hush, Ty," the girl said. Then, with a shy, beautiful smile, she added, "I hope your brother will be okay."

"Thanks."

"Joshua?" his father called out. "I'll be needin' you now, *boo*."

The little one tilted his head. *"Boo?"*

"It means 'son' in our language. In Pennsylvania Dutch."

His father's voice deepened. "Joshua, *now*."

Looking at the girl, Josh shrugged. "I'm sorry. I must go."

"I know," she murmured.

The older boy rolled his eyes. With a slight smirk, he spoke. "Guess you've got to go saddle up your horse, huh?"

Since that was most likely what he was going to have to do, Josh said nothing, just turned and walked away.

These new neighbors weren't like the Wilsons at all.

"I can't believe you were flirting with that guy," Charlie said to Lilly as soon as they squeezed through the thick hedge and were back on their own driveway. Ty had already scampered on ahead, no doubt eager to report back to their mom everything that had just happened.

Oh, how their little brother loved to report anything he could to their parents.

"I was not flirting," Lilly retorted, though she felt her face burn with embarrassment. "I was just being nice. You could have been a little bit nicer, too, Charlie."

"Why? I don't want to be their friends."

"You should. They're our neighbors."

"Not mine. Well, not mine for long. I'm going back to college, remember? By August I'll be out of Sugarcreek for good."

"How can I forget?" College was all Charlie ever talked about. When their parents had decided that they were going to leave Cleveland and move to Sugarcreek at the end of the semester, they'd also told Charlie he was going to have to take the spring semester off from college. He'd been taking classes at a nearby community college and living at home. Now he was working nonstop at a dry cleaners in town so he could pay for his room and board at Bowling Green University in the fall.

Charlie never missed an opportunity to remind Lilly that it was her fault his whole life had been turned upside down. Somewhere along the way he'd started acting like he knew everything, too. Lilly was sick of him.

23

Of course, at the moment, she was sick of everyone. And morning sick. And sick in her heart. She wondered if pregnancy did that to a person.

"Hopefully, we won't have to see them much," Charlie said, focusing on their Amish neighbors again. "Did you see that guy's hair?" He sneered. "It looked like someone stuck a bowl on his head. And can you imagine having to drive around a wagon all the time?"

"His hair was fine. And it's called a buggy, not a wagon."

"Whatever." Charlie shook his head in derision. "If I was him, I would've run so far away from here."

"Oh, stop. I don't know why you have to always spout off your opinions, Charlie."

"I'm 'spouting them off' because I'm right. You should have listened to me when I warned you about Alec Wagoner."

She winced. Just hearing Alec's name sent a tremor of pain through her. "You played football with Alec. You never said a bad word about him before we started dating."

"I said enough," he retorted. "I told you he was selfish. I told you Alec only wanted one thing — and I was sure right about that." Looking way too superior, he looked

24

her over. "Now, think about the mess you're in."

"The mess I'm in? It's called being pregnant. And stop acting so shocked and high and mighty. It's not the nineteen fifties, you know."

With quick, efficient movements, Charlie picked up the bucket, towel, and sponges he'd been cleaning his truck with and placed them on the shelf in the garage. "You really ought to stop acting like you're so happy. Your *pregnancy* is why we all moved here. Your condition."

"I know that."

"Then you should know that it hasn't been easy, having to tell everyone we moved because of Dad's job. We all had to lie. All so you can have that baby and put it up for adoption without anyone back home finding out."

Lilly flinched. She turned her back on Charlie so he wouldn't see the tears forming in her eyes.

But then it didn't matter anyway. With three stomps, Charlie strode along the newly shoveled path into the house, letting the back door swing shut with a slam.

Lilly hugged her waist for comfort. Well, what was left of it. Now she was twelve weeks pregnant, and felt like her life was over.

Of course, as she thought of the state her family was in . . . of how no one ever talked about the baby — of how everyone only referred to the baby as "her condition" — she was miserable.

No one understood. Worse, no one even wanted to try.

Even though the air was cold and the ground was snow covered, she sank down on the wooden bench on the side of their driveway. As she swiped at a trail of tears on her cheek, she stared at the hedge and wondered about the family next door.

They were so different . . . but so not. The uproar over that little boy's fall wasn't that much different than how her mom had reacted when Ty had fallen off his bike and cut his hand on a glass bottle.

The two teenagers her age hadn't seemed all that different from Charlie and herself either. They'd looked irritated with the little guy, but like they cared about him, too. And the girl was pretty. Lilly knew plenty of girls back at her old high school who would have paid big money to have creamy perfect skin like she had.

Though she tried not to think about the older boy, Lilly couldn't help but think about him, too. His voice had been deep and a little husky. His body had looked so solid and strong.

He was really handsome.

But what she wasn't able to get out of her mind was the way he'd looked at her. He'd had such wonder in his eyes — such admiration . . . for a brief moment, she felt pretty again. Almost like herself.

Almost like the person she used to be.

CHAPTER 2

"That will be forty-seven dollars and eighty-four cents," Joshua said to the pair of tourists who'd just brought two baskets and an assortment of Amish-made jams to the cash register. After they handed him three twenties, he carefully counted out their change, then handed them their purchases.

"Thank you so much," one of the ladies said. "We just love your store."

"I'm glad you do," he replied. "Please visit us again."

After they picked up their purchases, Joshua watched them go with a bit of bemusement. The women had spent a good hour in his family's store, examining quilts and reading cookbooks. They were some of the customers he liked best — ones who looked like they truly enjoyed all the merchandise his family worked so hard to acquire and display.

The ladies' departure brought a momentary quiet to the front of the store — and allowed Joshua's mind to drift to things of a more personal nature.

To Gretta.

Lately, Gretta had become much quieter around him. He knew she was still fretting about their argument. And still wondering why he'd gotten so upset with her for talking to her friend about wedding plans.

He wasn't quite sure himself. Usually, he appreciated the way she'd never hidden her feelings for him. He often chuckled when he heard that she was daydreaming about their life together. After all, Judith had spoken plenty of times about how she planned to set up housekeeping. It was what girls did.

But lately he'd been feeling trapped in his life. Trapped about his lack of choices. He'd started thinking about how everyone was practically counting the days until he and Gretta were to be married. His lack of excitement about that worried him. Led him to think that maybe they weren't suited to each other, after all.

Of course, even considering such a selfish thing was shameful. He was a lucky man to have such a girl as his sweetheart. Many a man, both young and old, had told him he was blessed to have found such a modest,

29

devout girl.

She was pretty, too. Gretta had long brown hair the color of black walnut and the most expressive blue eyes. Light and cloudy and mesmerizing — as if a world of thoughts were hidden just underneath her serene exterior.

He knew he was lucky. Just lately, though, he wished his heart felt as pleased to see her as his head knew he should be.

He'd known Gretta Hershberger all his life. From the moment their teacher had asked him to help her learn to skate, she'd been near. She was shy, yes. But she was also smart and good-natured.

Usually, he'd accepted that working at the store and one day marrying Gretta would be his future. But now he was wondering if there might be another woman in the world who would suit him just as much. Or a bit better.

Though his brother Caleb had remarked that Joshua had been moony-eyed over their English neighbor, Joshua knew he wasn't even remotely thinking about jumping the fence. He was content to be Amish.

But he wasn't content with everything.

"Joshua, you gonna work today, son, or be waited on?" his father called out from his perch on top of a ladder.

"I'm working. Hey, Daed, step down off of there. I'll put the rest of the stock away on those top shelves."

Instead of looking pleased that his son was so thoughtful, his *daed* frowned. "Think I'm too old to be climbing ladders, do you?"

"Not so much. It's just that I'm younger, yes? And, well, Dr. Kiran has already patched one of us up. He probably doesn't want to see us again this week."

With a wry chuckle, his dad shook his head. "That Anson. I hope he gains some sense soon. That would be mighty nice," his daed quipped as he made his way down the rungs.

The way his father scampered up and down the ladders and such in the store, Joshua thought more than once that it was a fair miracle he'd never gotten hurt.

Knock wood, it was a blessing no one had ever gotten seriously injured. The Graber Country Store was a mammoth building, by most folks' estimation. Yet, it was a welcoming place, too. Inside, it smelled of apples and cinnamon and freshly oiled wood. Worn, thick planks of wood covered the floor, and the years had marked their way. Nicks and divots pockmarked the once smooth planks, showing one and all that this was a place of business and gathering.

31

Just as he prepared to carry some baskets to the top, he spotted Gretta.

"Take a moment for Gretta now, son," his daed murmured, before making his way back to the front counter where Judith was ringing up customers. "You know she came here to see ya."

The gentle reminder flustered Joshua. His father was right — Gretta was too good a girl to be dodging. But what he didn't know was if she'd actually come to the store looking for him.

These days, nothing felt certain anymore.

As she walked a little closer, studying the shelves like she knew nothing about spices and the like, Josh dutifully set his armful down and strode over to her. *"Gut tawg, Gretta."*

She turned to him and almost smiled. "Good day to you, too, Joshua. I see you're here, working hard today."

"Where else would I be?" The moment his words were out, he wished he could take them back.

"I don't know." Biting her lip, she picked up a bottle of cinnamon and studied it instead of him. And, instead of teasing him like she used to, bright pink spots stained her cheeks. "I guess once again, I spoke without thinking."

Immediately embarrassed, he swallowed hard. "Did . . . did you need some help?"

"No, not really." Tucking her chin down slightly, she gave him a winsome look — one that until recently had set his heart to racing. "I only came in to get a few things for my mother." Looking into the sturdy woven basket hanging on her arm, she said, "So far, I've got popcorn and butter and cheese. Oh, but I do need some yarn, if you have any."

"We do. Yards and yards of yarn," he said, making a little joke. But when she didn't so much as smile, he cleared his throat. "Here, I'll help you."

"Oh. Yes, thank you. I'd like that." She treated him to a strained smile. She paused momentarily, obviously waiting for him to carry her basket. Joshua did just that. However, a small part of him was again irritated with her. Gretta always expected things from him. Always. And until lately, he'd always done what she wanted.

"Would you like to come over for dinner tonight? We're having roast chicken."

"I don't think I can. I'm due to work till close today."

"But what about afterward? I'm bringing a pie home from work. I made coconut pies

33

today at the inn. I know that's your favorite."

Coconut pie was his absolute favorite, and Gretta Hershberger made a pie like no other. "I do like your coconut pie."

"So do you want to come over, then?"

"I . . . all right. *Danke*."

When a fresh look of relief crossed her features, Josh felt a flutter of foreboding.

Was this how their life together would always be? With him watching his words so he didn't hurt her feelings by mistake? Always doing her bidding because it would be easier than making her sad? No surprises? Nothing new and different?

The idea was enough to give a man a moment's pause.

When the front door jingled, he left Gretta's side with some relief. Concentrating on work was far more preferable than reflecting on the state of things with Gretta.

"Can I help ya?" he asked, then was brought up short when he saw who the customer was.

"You can," his neighbor said. "Hi, again. I'm Lilly."

"Hi. I'm Joshua."

"I just ran in for milk. I'm running errands for my mother."

He pointed to the wall behind him, where

34

a long row of refrigerator cases were. "There's milk there."

"Thanks," she said, turning quickly enough to flutter the curls around her face.

With some dismay, he caught himself staring. Abruptly, he faced the cash register. It wouldn't do for anyone to see him staring after Lilly like an infatuated schoolboy.

Because at the moment, that was exactly what he was feeling like.

Sometime later, after Lilly had left with her milk and Gretta had left with her things, Joshua slipped on his thick leather gloves and began unboxing and arranging the latest inventory. The hard work felt good, and it served to keep his hands and mind busy enough so that he wouldn't be focused on Gretta.

When Caleb sauntered in to help after his day at the Amish school, Joshua only grunted. He didn't feel like talking to his chatty brother and hoped Caleb would get the message.

"I passed our new neighbors today when I was walking here from the schoolhouse," Caleb said as he pulled open a large container of oatmeal. Their customers liked buying bulk items in smaller quantities, so it was a constant job to divide the grains and beans into family-sized portions. "You wantin' one pound bags today, Joshua?"

"One pound is *gut*."

Caleb pulled over the scale, a roll of plastic bags, and the container of rubber bands. Like he'd done so many times before, he flicked open a plastic bag, poured a good amount of oatmeal inside, then carefully added spoonfuls at a time until it weighed precisely one pound. "Anyway, I guess I should say that they passed me."

"Who? The Allens?"

In the way only a fifteen-year-old could, Caleb rolled his eyes. "Well, *jah*. I told you I was talkin' about the neighbors. Anyway, I think it was the older boy and his sister who I saw. Charlie and Lilly are their names. Charlie and Lilly Allen."

Before Joshua could mention that he'd seen Lilly in the store, his brother whistled low. "You should have seen how that truck could go."

Unlike Caleb and Anson, the luxury of an automobile had never interested him too much. "I've seen trucks before."

"I know." He shrugged as he fastened the bag with the rubber band, then flicked open another plastic sack. "But this boy's was loud and fast. Since the sun was out and it was forty degrees out, their windows were down. They were playing music, too. The sister — *Lilly* — she had her head back against the seat and was laughing and singing." Caleb's lips twitched. "It was a fair sight to see and hear."

Recalling how mesmerized he'd been by her curls just an hour earlier, Joshua imagined it had been a fair sight, indeed.

Still thinking about the truck, Caleb grinned. "One day I'm aiming to take a truck out for a spin."

Joshua figured Caleb would. He'd just begun his running-around time and seemed eager to experience as many English things as possible. Though their parents did their best to pretend Caleb wasn't out with his friends till late at night, Joshua remembered his *rumspringa* clearly enough to keep careful tabs on him.

Joshua had never done too much during his running-around time. Mostly, he'd just enjoyed the extra time with his friends and the opportunity to be a bit more lazy.

But, for a brief moment, Joshua felt tempted, just like Caleb. It would be something to be sitting next to Lilly Allen and watch her curly hair fly every which way in the wind.

"I wonder if her hair gets in knots, flying like that," he mused.

"What?" Caleb stared at him in surprise.

"Oh, nothing." Joshua tried to look bored again. "I mean, I hope they'll have a care. They could hurt someone, going so fast down the roads. Especially in the evening. Think of the Yoders' grandfather. He still takes out his buggy from time to time."

"If Mr. Yoder gets injured, I doubt it will be the Allen's fault. That *alter* is near blind, and his horse is, too. And, he's as cranky as an old saw."

"That is true." The old Mr. Yoder was a mite difficult to be around.

Scooping oatmeal again, Caleb continued. "Anyway, maybe one day, when we all get to know one another better, the boy will take me out for a ride."

"I doubt that. He didn't look interested in knowing us."

"They will want to know us, one day," Caleb said confidently. "We're new and different, and that's always *gut*."

"Says who?"

"Says everyone. Your problem, Joshua, is that your life is all planned out."

He knew that. But he didn't need Caleb to know that, too. Making his voice brusque, he said, "What are you talking about?"

"You know exactly what you're gonna be doing the rest of your life, that's what I'm

38

saying. You're going to work here, marry Gretta, have a *boppli* or two, and raise them to work here at the store." Caleb grimaced. "Your future is so set it could be in cement."

"There's nothing wrong with that."

"I didn't say there was. I just . . . well, I just think it's a shame you never look around and wonder about things. I'm finding out that there's lots to see, you know."

"All I know is that I have to do so much around here because you're out looking too much. You arrive here late and try and sneak out early."

"Not all the time."

"Enough of it. And once here, you spend your time dreaming about trucks instead of getting work done."

"At least I dream, *bruder.* I think you've forgotten how."

Sometimes Joshua felt he'd forgotten, too. "Well, you best work harder otherwise we'll be here until dawn."

"And that would be a real shame, too." He winked. "Then you'd miss having pie with Gretta."

Turning to him in surprise, Joshua glared. "How'd you know about that?"

Caleb chuckled. "Because it's like I said, brother. You're as predictable as the sun . . . and twice as cool."

Joshua tried to pretend that he didn't care about being predictable. Tried to pretend that wasn't a problem for him at all.

But as he strode away from Caleb and got to work opening the next group of packages, he slumped. He was almost twenty years old and his life was set.

Maybe he should've done more during his *rumspringa,* like Caleb was doing now. Maybe he should've ridden in more fast trucks and smiled at more pretty girls.

Maybe if he had, he wouldn't be so fretful now. Maybe if he had, he wouldn't be so curious about his neighbors. Maybe if he had, he'd be more taken with Gretta Hershberger.

CHAPTER 3

Ever since the new year had started, there'd been something terribly different about Joshua, Gretta decided as she slowly walked along the neatly shoveled sidewalk toward the Sugarcreek Inn the next morning. When he'd come over for pie, he'd seemed distant and curt.

Not like his usual self at all.

Oh, he'd smiled her way and complimented her cooking, but his eyes had looked as if they were miles away.

And when her parents had given them a few moments alone in the hearth room, he hadn't done or said a thing that was remotely loverlike. There they'd sat, side by side on the couch in front of the cozy, roaring fire. Shadows from the flames and the kerosene lamp cast a romantic spell over them both.

But instead of holding her hand or talking about their upcoming skating plans — the way he used to do — he'd merely held his black felt hat and looked as if he was counting the minutes until he could leave.

In fact, the only time he'd looked like he'd had any emotion in his expression had been when he'd talked of Anson's trip to the hospital — and his new neighbors' penchant for sleeping in on Saturdays.

When he'd said goodbye, he hadn't mentioned when he would see her again. Before, he'd always say that he'd see her at the inn, or that he'd see her at church. Or even that he and Jim were anxious to take her out for a buggy ride.

But he'd done none of that.

After depositing her cape and black bonnet on the hooks in the cloakroom of the Sugarcreek Inn, Gretta straightened her white prayer *kapp,* washed her hands, then joined her friend Miriam in the kitchen.

More often than not, they worked together, which suited Gretta just fine. Miriam made her smile, and was a good worker, too. When they were together, they accomplished a great many tasks with ease.

"So, are we still making cream pies today?"

"We are. Banana, peanut, and coconut." Miriam, being the type of girl she was, hardly looked up from the pie crust she was fluting. Time on the clock was time meant for working.

Usually Gretta felt the same way. But today she felt more empty than she could recall feeling in quite some time. As she got out a tray of eggs, a gallon of milk, and a box of cornstarch, she murmured, "Miriam, when you and your family visited the Graber's store the other day, did you notice anything different about Joshua?"

Miriam's raven black eyebrows wrinkled together. "No. Now that I think on it, I hardly talked with him at all, Gretta. And when we did, it was only about the pound of bacon I'd ordered. Why?"

"He's seemed *fremt* lately. Strange."

"Strange, how?" Eyes twinkling, Miriam leaned closer. "What did he do? Only stopped to speak with you for five minutes instead of the usual twenty?"

"It was more than that." Still stewing, Gretta slipped on her white apron, then joined her friend behind the counter of the large, old-fashioned kitchen where they'd worked together for over a year. "When he came over for pie last night, he hardly spoke. He left earlier than usual, too."

"Maybe he was tired."

"Maybe, but I don't think that was it." Though she knew it wouldn't come out

43

right, Gretta added, "It's been other things, too. When he walked me around the store, he looked as if he couldn't wait for me to leave." She was still too sad to tell Miriam about his anger during their buggy ride.

Ever practical, her girlfriend shrugged. "Like I said, I bet he was just busy or tired. My parents say that the Graber's store is doing a wonderful-*gut* business. Tourists have found the place, you know."

Up to her elbows in snowy white flour, Miriam rolled out another circle of golden dough as she continued. "Think of how it is when we're baking bread and people want to stop by to visit. It's hard to knead big batches of dough and be chipper at the same time."

Miriam did have a point. When their heads and bodies were working in unison, she and Miriam could slice and season and mash fillings for ten applesauce pies at a time . . . if they weren't interrupted.

But more often than not, someone was always leaning over the counter and wanting to chat through the picture window that separated the dining room from the vast kitchen. It was rarely the tourists who interrupted them, though. No, the tourists might stare a bit or ask hesitant questions. It was members of their community who liked to talk. The busybodies who had no fear of interrupting their workday.

After pulling down a large stainless steel pot, Gretta opened the refrigerator and took out whipping cream and butter. From the pantry, she brought out the rest of the items needed in order to make the base for their signature creamy coconut cream pies. After measuring out some portions and turning the range on, she got to thinking again. "I guess I'm being silly, just looking for trouble."

"Maybe so." Emptying out the last of the dough, Miriam rolled it into a fine ball, then began to form the last pie crust. "My mother says the person who goes looking for trouble will always find it. You've got a nice man courtin' you. You should be counting your blessings."

"You're right." Briefly, Gretta closed her eyes and tried to say a little prayer of thanks. But unlike old times, she didn't feel the immediate sense of peace that she usually did.

In spite of her best intentions, she couldn't forget the awkward silence that had hung in the air after their argument in the courting buggy. Though she and Joshua had never mentioned the episode, it had bothered her greatly. She had always promised herself that she'd never be in a situation like her parents. She'd always vowed never to live in a way where she was afraid to speak her mind.

But now she feared that life with Joshua might be filled with moments just like that.

That evening, after helping her mother with the dishes and her younger sister Margaret hem a new dress, Gretta sought refuge in her room.

Sometimes, it was difficult to keep her usual serene and calm demeanor. Her mother talked like a magpie, always chirping about Gretta's future with Joshua. As usual, her father said little, seemingly content to keep the women's conversations to the women.

And Margaret, well, she was on the cusp of adulthood. Now that she was fifteen and in her last year of school, she was preparing herself for other learnings . . . how to manage a *gut* home and cook and can and garden and sew. All things every Amish girl looked forward to doing one day for a man of her own.

As for herself, Gretta didn't feel especially excited about her future. While Gretta had always found Joshua to be one of the handsomest boys in the order, and he'd made her heart flutter since she'd first skated with

46

him long ago, she was beginning to wonder. Was that enough to build a life together? Lately, they'd had little to talk about. The increasingly awkward silences that rose between them were troubling. It surely didn't bode well for a happy home life.

And oh, but how she hoped for a happy home.

Sometimes she wished the Lord would be just a little more forthcoming about his desires for her. Or at the least, she wished He would have crossed their paths at a later date. Then she'd know for sure that Joshua was the right man for her.

That she wasn't simply settling.

After pulling off her boots, Gretta curled up on top of the quilt and breathed deep. Now she had the peace and quiet she loved and needed. Now she would be able to pray to her Father and hear his advice.

After exhaling, she sat as still and quiet as she could and closed her eyes. Just like she always did.

Then, opening her mind, Gretta began to pray. She prayed for her family and gave thanks for her friends and her home and her many gifts. Then, almost tentatively, she ventured her questions.

Father, why are all our plans turning topsy-turvy? What am I supposed to be learning

47

from this?

Gretta inhaled as she waited to hear His will. Opening her eyes, she looked around the room, centered herself, then tried again.

Father, I'm truly grateful for everything, but is Joshua really my intended? Have our troubles started because we're not meant to be together?

Minutes passed as she waited quietly for the feeling of peace usually provided whenever she reached out to Him. His reply. But once again, none came. What was wrong?

Feeling at a loss, Gretta looked at the other bed in the room, the other twin-sized bed with the matching quilt to her own.

Beth's bed.

After all this time, to still refer to the bed as her sister's was a foolish habit. Beth had been gone for ten years.

But even though she was gone in body, Gretta still liked the idea of her sister sharing a room with her.

Beth's bout with pneumonia had taken them all by surprise. At first, they'd all simply thought she'd had a bad cold. It was only after her skin had grown a shade gray that her parents had hired an *Englischer* to take them to the hospital.

Not two days later, she'd died.

When her parents had returned, they'd

become different people. It was like all their own joy and happiness had faded when their oldest child had passed on to heaven. Gretta hated to think anything unkind about Beth, but the truth was, Beth had been no tiny saint. Even at age ten she'd been bossy. Always something of a know-it-all, though Gretta figured every older sister tended to be that way.

But she missed her terribly. Gretta had a feeling that these days Beth — in her usual bossy way — would have had lots to say about their parents' rocky marriage, about Josh's inattention . . . and most of all about Gretta's waiting around for him to become baptized and propose.

A tiny knock interrupted her musings. "Gretta, can I come in?"

"Sure."

Margaret peeked around the door. When Gretta noticed that her sister was in something of a frenzy, she said, "What's wrong?"

"Mamm and Daed won't let me go to the singin' on Sunday."

"Why ever not?"

She frowned. "They say it's because I haven't been doing my chores well enough."

This was not an unusual occurrence. Feeling like a bossy older sister herself, Gretta tried to impart a little bit of wisdom.

49

Something that Beth might have said if she was there in body, too. "You haven't been doing your chores well at all."

"I have, too."

"You haven't, Margaret, and you know I'm right. You rush through everything like the house is on fire."

As usual, Margaret ignored the criticism and pointed out her needs. "But Micah will be at the singing. I can't bear to miss him."

"If you don't see him then you'll see him another time."

"You're just saying that because you forget what it's like to want to be with someone special."

"I don't think I've forgotten that at all."

Looking at her with a bit of disdain, Margaret rolled her eyes. "If you're talking about you and Joshua, I don't think you're feeling the same way that I do about Micah."

"And why is that?"

"Because I'm happy when I'm with Micah. I feel so happy that sometimes I wonder if my heart is going to beat too fast! You never look that way when you're with Joshua."

Her stomach sunk. Gretta hadn't realized that others had been noticing the changes in her relationship with Joshua, too. But as

50

bad as things were, she wasn't ready to admit that to her little sister. "I am happy with Joshua."

"You may be happy, but you don't feel as strongly as I do about Micah. When the two of you are together, you act like an old married couple."

"We do not." The criticism stung — as did the knowledge that her sister was probably right. Sometimes it did seem as if she and Joshua had drifted far apart.

"The other day you two hardly talked at all . . . just like Mamm and Daed."

"I hardly think Joshua and I were acting like our parents." After all, their parents argued all the time.

Margaret raised her chin. "You two were closer than you might think."

"Perhaps," she said grudgingly. Now that she thought about it, she and Joshua's argument had been full of blame and accusations. Since then, they hadn't had much to say to each other. Everything had been different.

But that wasn't something she could share with anyone. "Was there anything else you were needin'?"

"Nope." Margaret flopped down on Beth's bed, just like she belonged there. Gretta tried not to let it bother her. After all, Margaret hardly remembered her oldest sister.

But still, Gretta resented Margaret's intrusion, especially since she was being so critical. She had so little time to herself, she cherished every moment of it.

And, well, she really did need some time to sort out how she was feeling. She knew from being around the Grabers that all marriages didn't simply collapse and turn into mere partnerships of bitter feelings. No, Joshua's family was boisterous and rowdy, and loving and giving, too. In her heart, Gretta knew that part of why she had looked to a future with Joshua was because she'd been eager to be surrounded by such love.

She needed to figure out why things between her and Joshua seemed so out of sorts. "If you're not needin' anything else, I think you should go on to bed."

"It's not that late."

"It's been dark for hours. It's late enough."

With a pouty glare Margaret finally slid off the quilt, wrinkling it in the process. "You sure are grumpy."

"I am not. I'm fine."

"Does it have to do with you and Joshua?"

"No." She closed her eyes, hoping that the good Lord wouldn't mind too much that she was lying so.

"Oh. Well, if you want to ever talk to somebody at singings besides Joshua, you should visit with Roland."

"Roland Schrock? Why?"

"He fancies ya, that's why."

"I don't think so." She tried to recall his behavior the last few times she'd visited with him. Roland was a different sort of fellow. Even tempered and always happy, Roland was easy to be around, but had never sparked her interest like Joshua had.

Truth was, ever since Joshua Graber had taught her to ice skate years ago, she'd never looked at another boy in a romantic way.

"Oh, he does like you. He fancies you something awful. I know I'm right about that." Pointing to her eyes, Margaret smiled knowingly. "While you've been all moony-eyed over Joshua, I've seen things you don't."

"Such as?"

"Roland watches you nonstop whenever you're in his company. He always has."

The words were troubling. She didn't want to like anyone else, or for anyone else to fancy her. She wanted Joshua to like her and for her to feel like they were meant to be together. She didn't want to worry about their arguments and the chills in their relationship. She wanted a marriage with

53

Joshua like his parents' marriage seemed to be. She wanted a relationship that was warm and loving and easy. She yearned for a home that was a shelter from the world.

She wanted a relationship with her husband that was the complete opposite of how her parents talked to each other.

But she would never tell anyone that.

"Good night, Margaret," she said, her voice a little more sharp than usual. "Don't forget to say your prayers."

"I always say them, sister," Margaret said over her shoulder as she exited the room.

When she was alone again, Gretta pondered Margaret's words. Had the Lord sent her sister in with that piece of news about Roland for a reason? Was He intending for her to spend some time thinking about other beaus?

If that was the case, what was she going to do about Joshua? And her parents? They always talked about what a *gut* daughter she was because she'd never caused them trouble.

She'd never experimented with English ways like others did during their *rumspringa.* She'd already been baptized . . . she'd been eager to join the church.

She'd been eager to marry Joshua and start her life with him.

54

But now things seemed so jumbled that she fretted she was about to disappoint a great many people.

And maybe even God himself.

CHAPTER 4

Being homeschooled was boring. It was also really hard, if no matter how hard you tried, you still couldn't do Algebra II. Frustrated, Lilly called out, "Mom, I just don't understand what I'm supposed to do with this algebraic equation."

Her mom looked up from the mail she was sorting. "Don't ask me. I stopped being able to help you after sixth grade."

"But I need to get it done. I'm so far behind."

"Charlie will help you when he gets home from work."

"But he's not going to want to help. You know he won't." Tentatively, she said, "Maybe I should just go to the local high school."

"In your condition? I don't think so."

"I'm pregnant, Mom. I don't have the flu. It's not catching."

Her mother's expression tightened. "Don't

56

joke about this. Believe me, dear, you don't want to be the focus of all that gossip."

Lilly had started thinking that even facing gossip would be better than spending every single day alone. "Joking about it is pretty much all I can do. Everyone in this house likes to pretend I'm not pregnant."

"We just don't want to dwell on something that can't be changed." Pushing the pile of magazines and bills aside, her mother turned to face her directly. "That reminds me, have you been looking at the notebook the adoption agency brought over?"

"No." Lilly hated that notebook. It was filled with sweet letters to both her and her baby, telling all about how much every family wanted a baby. How much they wanted her baby.

How they wanted her to choose them. To get to know them. Let them take her out for coffee or ice cream. To see the nursery they already had decorated.

All of it gave her the willies.

"Ms. Vonn from the adoption agency will be by at the end of the week. She's a busy lady and is going to expect some answers. You really ought to narrow the choices."

"I know."

After leveling a slow look her way, her

mom nodded. "Good. I'm glad you know that."

Lilly stared at her math book again. Even looking at that was better than meeting her mother's demanding gaze.

Her mom stood up and carried the mail to a basket. As always, everything had a place in the kitchen. She looked over her shoulder. "After, uh, everything . . . we'll be able to start picking out a college for you. Just like we did for Charlie. Then, next thing you know, you'll be thinking about college classes and maybe even a dorm and room-mates. Everything's going to be terrific then."

Because then her parents will have been able to forget that she'd ever been pregnant at all.

And though she'd regretted saying yes to Alec instead of saving herself for marriage, she had come to terms with the baby grow-ing inside of her. She'd already started to love it. "Mom, what if maybe I don't want to give the baby up?"

"That's not even open for discussion." In three short steps, her mother pulled on yel-low gloves and took hold of a frying pan that had been soaking. "We already decided you would," she said over the scrubbing.

"Maybe I changed my mind." When her

mother paused in mid-scrub, Lilly tilted her head up. "Maybe I don't want to hand my baby over to strangers."

The pan clattered in the sink. "Don't be ridiculous. Those people won't be strangers if you ever got to know them. Plus, you'll get to see that baby whenever you want with this open adoption you asked for."

"I know, but —"

"Lilly, why are you even thinking about such things? Everything's already been decided. Alec was fine with that."

"Alec is a jerk. Of course he's not ready to be a parent. But, Momma, maybe I am."

For a moment, her mother's eyes softened. It was so rare that Lilly ever called her momma anymore. But then her expression hardened. "That's childish thinking." In a series of hasty movements, her mother turned off the faucet and yanked off both yellow rubber gloves. "You're eighteen, Lilly. Only eighteen. You're definitely not ready to raise a child. Being a parent involves more than simply giving birth, you know."

"I know. But maybe I am ready to be a mom." Her stomach fluttered. Feeling the movement, Lilly pressed her hands over her stomach. Maybe it was the baby. Maybe it was just nerves. But no matter what, Lilly couldn't deny that it was *her* body that was going through all the changes. Her body, not her mother's.

She was the one who had gotten pregnant.

"Think of the consequences, Lilly," her mother said, coming to sit by her side. "I love you dearly, and I want you to be happy. I want you to do all the things you've planned. Think how much your life would change if you had a child."

"My life's already changed," she retorted, amazed that her mother could be so blind. "I've lost my boyfriend. I've moved away from all my best friends . . . and, oh, yeah. My family treats me like I'm a slut."

"Lillian Rose! Don't talk like that."

"Why, Mom? It's true. Everyone in this house wants this baby to go away. You all either constantly remind me of 'my mistake' . . . or you talk about how good life is going to be once 'this episode is over with.' Well, maybe I don't want it to be over."

"You don't have a choice. We already spent hours talking about this."

"But —"

"That's enough." Reaching out, her mother clasped both of her hands. "Now, this is what we're going to do. First, we're not going to mention any of these crazy ideas to your father. He's got enough to worry about, with his new job at the phone company. Next, you are going to work on your algebra homework and then you're going to pick out three couples who you'd like to interview."

"But —"

"There's no discussion, Lillian. We're out of choices. We're out of options." Softening her voice, she gently squeezed her shoulders. "I promise, this is for the best. Every baby deserves to grow up in a house full of love. By two parents who will love him or her. Don't be so selfish."

Lilly's mother walked out of the kitchen, leaving Lilly staring at the open math book, with a burning sensation in the pit of her stomach.

Was she being selfish? Did she really want this baby, now? This baby that she'd never intended to have in the first place?

As the adoption notebook stared right back at her, Lilly knew she'd never felt more miserable in her entire life. Or more alone.

Even in the coldest days of winter, there was no escaping the chores that had to be done. After breaking the thin layer of ice covering the top of the horses' troughs, Joshua filled each with fresh water and oats.

Next came the cleaning of the stalls, which

Anson should've been helping him do, if he hadn't been foolish enough to break his arm. And, as usual, Caleb was no where to be found, either.

Joshua wrapped the thick navy scarf Gretta had knitted for him for Christmas a bit more securely around his neck. Back when he'd received the scarf, he'd been sure no one could make him happier.

Now things seemed different. But was it all because of the English family next door? Because of Lilly? Could one girl really change his way of thinking so drastically?

That was a sad thing if it was true.

Feeling more disgruntled than ever, he grimly began raking away the soiled hay in Jim's stall. At first his muscles burned in protest. Now that it was twilight, the barn had turned colder. Each swipe felt heavy and awkward. But soon he was moving well, like he always did.

He'd just spread fresh hay on the floor of the last stall when Caleb finally showed up. Unable to hide his irritation, Joshua glared. "*Bruder,* where have you been? I've been doing all of this by myself. I coulda used your help, you know."

Caleb didn't look the least bit apologetic. "I was over at the Allens."

Joshua was stunned. "Doing what?"

"Retrieving Anson, that's what." Crossing his mittened arms across his chest, Caleb slouched against one of the stalls like he had nothing to do but stand and chat. "Anson wandered over there this afternoon and was taking his time coming back. Mamm got worried."

"I hadn't realized Anson knew them."

"Anson knows everyone, you know that. He wandered over there to meet their youngest, Ty."

"And how did they get along?"

"About how you'd expect. They're nine and ten, after all."

Joshua didn't know why he was surprised. The younger a person was, the less it seemed differences mattered.

However, there was a time not so long ago when he could never imagine any Amish *kinner* spending a moment at an *Englischer*'s house. But now that both the Amish and the English worked so much together in the Sugarcreek community, the lines between their worlds were not near so finely drawn. Though the Graber family was firmly planted in the Amish way of life, their father, Frank, had often said he was smart enough to realize that no good would come from ignoring everyone else. Especially since he owned one of the busiest stores in the town.

Still not eager to abandon his annoyance for having to do most of the chores by himself, Joshua said, "And how are things at the Allens? Did you even get a chance to speak to them, or did you simply claim Anson and leave?"

"They are good." With a secret smile, he motioned behind him. "Lilly followed us back, by the way."

Joshua dropped the rake as Lilly stepped through the open doorway and into view. Her wide, dark brown eyes and flushed cheeks signaled that she'd heard every complaining word that he'd uttered.

"Hi," she said with a tiny smile. "I'm sorry to ruin your evening."

"I . . . uh . . . you didn't."

"Are you sure? You sound busy."

Oh, he could wring Caleb's neck for embarrassing him like this! To Lilly, he gentled his voice. "Come in from the cold," he said, then found himself blushing. It surely wasn't much warmer in the barn than outside. And it smelled ripe of cow manure, too. "That is, if you don't mind the animals."

"I don't." Holding a pan in between her two hands, she said, "I brought over a cake, warm from the oven. Since Caleb had to make sure Anson didn't slip on any icy patches of snow or ice, I volunteered to carry it."

"That was mighty kind of you." Joshua felt his blush deepen. Oh, he had no skills in social talk like this. Nor was he used to feeling so self-conscious. With Gretta, he'd always felt secure and in charge.

This girl, on the other hand, did strange things to his pulse and his tongue. He felt completely tongue-tied at the moment.

Well, at least he could get rid of his pesky brother. "Caleb, *komm.* Take the cake and bring it inside to Mamm."

For once, Caleb didn't argue. Instead, he went to Lilly as Joshua asked, then took the warm pan to their house, pot holders and all.

As he darted off, Lilly stepped into the barn's shelter a bit more. Rubbing her arms briskly, she shivered. "It does feel better in here. The wind is awful today. Even my coat doesn't seem to do much good."

Her white coat fit her closely and ended just short of her hips. He wondered if she'd been thinking of warmth when she'd purchased it. "*Jah.* I mean, yes. Yes, the wind is fierce."

She smiled before turning away. Luckily, she had enough sense to step over a pile of soiled hay instead of walking right through it. "Can I see your horses?"

"Sure. They're right there."

"No, I mean, can I go up to them? Is it okay?"

"It's fine," he murmured from where he stood, choosing to keep his distance for a moment.

But that didn't stop him from watching her every move. With great interest he watched her smile at the horses, look in an empty stall, and wrinkle her nose at the smell. Finally, she stopped in front of Jim, their main workhorse. Jim was ten years old and a good horse. Easy of temperament and a good worker. His ears pricked up a bit when Lilly approached.

Joshua was just about to warn Lilly to have a care — to not do anything too fast or jerky around Jim, when she slowly pulled off her glove and placed her bare hand under the horse's nose. When Jim moved his head a bit, as if he were nodding permission, she smiled and tentatively patted his nose.

"I may not look like it, but I've been around horses a time or two," Lilly said with a smile. "My mom let me have horseback riding lessons when I was ten. Those didn't last long, but I still love horses."

66

"I . . . I like horses, too," he murmured, then closed his eyes as he heard his voice stumble and squeak. There was something about her that made him nervous, he couldn't deny that.

Joshua noticed that Jim looked to be plenty in love himself. The silly horse edged closed to the stall's door and craned his head so she could scratch his neck.

Lilly complied with a laugh.

Joshua simply stared, spellbound. Lilly's easy cheerfulness was so sweet, so fresh, he felt renewed in her presence. Almost like the Lord had dropped an angel in his barn to take away his cares and worries.

When she looked his way again, he cleared his throat. "I'm sorry you heard me grumble so much. I've been having to do both my brothers' work — Caleb's and Anson's. Sometimes I resent it."

"I know all about doing siblings' chores. Ty tries to get out of anything and everything." Still scratching Jim, she said, "What chores need to be done in here?"

"Tending to Jim, of course."

She looked around. "Jim?"

"That there is him."

When she still looked confused, his mouth went dry as he fumbled for the right words. For any right word. "Jim is the horse."

"Ah." Her hand paused. "Do you mind me petting him?"

"Not at all. He likes the attention, don'tcha think?" Jim looked as if he'd invite her right into his stall if he had the words.

She smiled. "I do." As the sun continued to fall outside, the light in the barn dimmed, making the conversation seem even more intimate. Lilly, in her jeans, green sweater, and form-fitting white jacket seemed to shine the brightest.

Not that he should be thinking about her in any way at all.

Searching for something to say, Joshua said, "I better warn you, if Anson enjoyed being at your house this afternoon, he'll be back again."

"Ty was glad to see him. He still hasn't made too many new friends at school."

"Well, Anson has yet to meet a stranger."

She chuckled. "We got that idea. He's really friendly."

"It's his way." Yes, it had always been Anson's way to be open and carefree. Perhaps because of his experiences at the store, or simply because of who the Lord had made him to be — he'd never had the natural reticence that had always plagued Josh.

When he spied Lilly looking at him thoughtfully, he knew he had to at least try to make more of an effort to befriend her. She was, after all, standing in his barn. "Um . . . what about you?"

"What about me what?"

"Have you been happy in Sugarcreek?"

To Joshua's surprise, a bit of her happiness seemed to float away. "I . . . I suppose."

Feeling embarrassed for asking such a personal question, Joshua simply nodded.

She took his silence as an invitation to explain herself. "We're still getting used to things here, you know. It's not just being around the Amish. It's living in a small town, too. It's a pretty big change."

Caleb returned just then with a big smile and Lilly's two pot holders. "My mother says *danke,* and if you'd like, you may come in and taste your cake."

Lilly laughed. "Now, wouldn't that just be the rudest thing? I don't expect to eat the treat I brought for your family." Wrapping her scarf back around her neck, she pulled her coat tighter around her chest. "I better get going anyway." With a little wave, she said goodbye then nimbly hopped over a pile of hay that had fallen.

Joshua hardly moved as he watched her dart out the barn door, then scamper over their field to the gap in between their two hedges. She moved so easily, she looked like a deer in spring. Free and easy.

By his side, Caleb watched her go. "She sure is a different sort a girl, don'tcha think?"

"Jah."

When Joshua didn't say any more, Caleb cleared his throat. "Sorry I was so late gettin' here. My time ran away from me."

"It's all right."

"It is? Oh." With a wary expression, Caleb bent down and picked up the rake. "It was nice over there. When I arrived, Mr. Allen was reading the paper and Mrs. Allen was making chicken and frosting that cake."

"Sounds like our home."

"It was like our home. Well, more or less. 'Course, they had every light on in that kitchen. And Mrs. Allen's chicken was stuffed in something Ty called a slow cooker." As he scooped up the soiled hay and put it in the ready wheelbarrow, Caleb chuckled. "I don't know how slow it was, though, you know?"

Caleb's prattling drew Joshua back to the present. "Maybe slow for the English."

"Maybe. Anyways, I tell ya, Anson in his plain clothes surely looked like a sore thumb sittin' next to Ty. That boy had a red and blue sweatshirt on with cartoons all over it. It was something to see."

"Anson said he liked it there?"

"Of course. He likes most everyone, you know." After cheerfully tossing a thatch of hay in the barrow and scooping up another rake full, Caleb chuckled as he picked up the wheelbarrow and directed it out the door. "We might end up being friends with our new neighbors after all. Who knows, maybe this time it will be the folks in that house who cross the hedge to attend a wedding."

His wedding with Gretta. "Maybe. Maybe so."

After putting the rake away, Joshua picked up a curry comb and began to brush Jim, thick and matted with a winter coat. As Jim nickered and tossed his head, Joshua couldn't help but smile. The horse didn't look too charmed by his touch.

"I don't blame ya, boy," Joshua murmured. He, too, thought the barn seemed a fair shade darker now that the neighbor girl had left.

CHAPTER 5

She and Joshua had skated together dozens of times, and each one had been fun — but Gretta felt sure that no time would ever be as special as their very first. Oh, but that first outing on the ice had been *wonderbaar!* So memorable.

If she closed her eyes, she could still recall the crisp smell of the pines nearby. The feel of the cold wind on her cheeks. The sense that something in her life was about to change, that for the first time, she'd made an important step toward adulthood.

Nothing since had been as special as that moment.

She and Joshua had been thirteen and fourteen and had competed in spelling bees and arithmetic drills for years. She'd taken to helping him with his cursive. He'd helped her with her reading English. Then one winter day their teacher, Miss Millersburg, announced that they would be stopping school an hour early so they could all go skating in the pond just over the grassy hill from their whitewashed schoolhouse.

Everyone had cheered except for Gretta. She knew how to skate, but not very well. Her mother had always found other things for her and Margaret to do at home instead of playing on the ice.

Little Margaret always found ways to sneak out of her obligations and do what she wanted, but Gretta never had. She'd known her mother's hesitance stemmed from Beth's death. Every snowfall and ice storm would create a look of fear on her mother's face and strict admonitions to take care in the cold.

So while everyone scampered to the small storage building near the pond, haggled over the assortment of skates — or pulled out their own — Gretta held back. She'd not been eager to slip and fall in front of everyone else.

But then Joshua had appeared by her side as she'd trudged up the hill, each foot feeling heavy and uncomfortable in her mother's thick boots. "You happy to be skating, Gretta?"

"Not so much. I don't know how to skate well," she'd confided.

Instead of teasing her, he'd taken her comment seriously. "That's all right. I'll help you get better. Stay with me and I'll make sure you don't fall."

He'd been true to his word. While everyone else was racing across the shiny glassy surface, he'd stayed by her side and gently coaxed her to keep her balance. When others played tag, he'd taught her to glide instead of choppily pushing one foot in front of the other. When the other boys got out sticks and a puck and asked him to join them in a quick game of hockey, he'd shaken his head and refused. "I'm skatin' with Gretta today," Joshua had stated each time.

By the time Gretta had unlaced her skates and set them back in the cold storage area, she'd had a terrible crush on Joshua Graber.

Until recently, those feelings hadn't dimmed much over the years. Joshua was handsome and well liked. His family was a good one, too. They'd always treated her like part of the family.

Actually, they treated her like she was Joshua's intended.

Everyone in their circle of friends, especially the other girls, thought Gretta was right lucky, indeed. Joshua was a nice person, and had a promising future, working in his family's wonderful-*gut* general

74

store. Their future was bright.

Had been bright. Now it felt a bit cloudy and dark.

Today, as they slowly glided along the perimeter of the snowy pond they knew so well, with only a few other skaters for company, Gretta began to wonder if maybe things between them weren't settled at all. Once again, Joshua kept turning away from her, like he was distracted.

And as for herself, well, she wondered if maybe her mind was gone running too much, too.

So far, every topic of conversation had been met with one-word answers or worse — had been ignored. Feeling determined, she made up her mind to capture his attention again. Perhaps the best course would be to bring up the past?

"Joshua, remember the first time we skated here together?"

"I do." Finally, taking a moment, he looked at her directly. "Miss Millersburg let school out early."

"I don't know what I would have done if you hadn't helped me so much that day." Hoping to surprise a smile from him, she gently prodded. "I was so grateful."

"It was a fun day."

Though she didn't need any help now, she

reached for his strong arm and clasped it. Just to feel like she had a hold on him. "You know what? I've always wondered why you helped me that day. All the other boys were playing hockey."

"Someone had to help ya," he said, finally looking at her the way he used to — with fondness and a gentle gleam in his eyes. "Plus Miss Millersburg had asked if I'd stay by your side. I couldn't *verra* well say no, now could I?"

She felt as if the bottom was falling out of her stomach. "You didn't ask me on your own?"

All this time she'd only imagined he'd sought her out?

Joshua's face froze as if he was realizing that he'd just relayed a secret she should have never known. "I would have wanted to ask you, though. I was afraid you'd say no."

"Oh. Well, um, do you still like skating with me?"

"I do. I mean, I would if we'd ever start moving our feet again. Let's get started, okay? It's mighty cold just standing here like statues."

"All right." Dropping his arm, she concentrated on gliding one foot in front of the other, but all the joy she used to feel was rapidly diminishing.

76

Something was missing from Joshua's expression. From the way he spoke to her. Why, it was like he was looking at her with one eye, but imagining someone else with the other.

She smiled gamely at a few school children who skated nearby, the brims of girls' black bonnets gently swaying with their movements. She remembered being that age . . . It had been a time of tumultuous emotions. She'd been eager to make friends and flirt, and yet there had always been a dark cloud over her spirits. Every year that passed brought with it a realization that Beth had never reached that age. As she heard a shout, she was bolted back to the present. Something with Joshua wasn't quite right. Though her stomach was in knots, she said, "Are you still thinking about our fight the other day?"

"What fight?"

"The argument we had in the buggy, of course. When you got mad at me for talking to Miriam about girlish things."

Joshua stared at her for a moment in confusion before understanding dawned. "Gretta, that was no fight. I was just grumpy, that was all. I don't like everyone knowing my business."

"Oh. Well, we were just so quiet afterward."

He looked uncomfortable. "I've . . . I've noticed things between us haven't been the same, too. But I'm not mad anymore."

"I was worried you still might be."

"That was weeks ago. Surely you don't think I'd still be worryin' about it. I can't imagine why you'd think that. I'm sorry you thought I was still mad."

An hour later, after they'd unlaced their skates and settled into the buggy, she attempted to be merry. "I, for one, will be glad to go to the restaurant and enjoy something warm to drink. Mrs. Kent makes the best hot cocoa."

Joshua said nothing.

She tried again. "We're about the same distance from the Sugarcreek Inn as from my place. Do you not want to go to the inn like we'd planned? If not, you could come over and we could just sit in the kitchen by ourselves. Would you like that better?"

Joshua looked into the distance and shook his head. He finally spoke. "I don't have time for hot cocoa today. It'd be best if I simply took you home."

"Oh. Well, all right." But it wasn't all right. They'd always had hot chocolate after skating. Used to be, Joshua had been reluctant to leave her side.

Still hardly looking at her, Joshua jiggled the reins. Jim pulled forward, the horse's breath causing little puffs of vapor to appear. "Maybe I'm getting tired of everything we always do," he said in spurts, like each word was getting pulled hard from his insides. "Maybe I'm wantin' to do something different."

Even with one of his mother's lovely 'round-the-world quilts tucked securely around her legs, Gretta felt ice cold. Each word was unwelcome and freezing her to the core. "Different, how?"

"I can't rightly say."

"Well, that makes no sense," she said practically. "You must have an idea, otherwise you wouldn't say such a thing."

"Never mind. I'm going to just take you home," he said again.

"And not come inside at all?"

"Not today."

"I see." But she didn't. She didn't see at all. Neither of them spoke as Jim brought them down a windy road, inside a covered bridge, and finally pulled down her lane. As they approached her home, Gretta noticed that only one light was burning. Her parents must not have expected them to come back; otherwise they usually set a cozy fire for her and Joshua in the family room.

Knowing that as soon as the buggy stopped on their driveway, her parents would be looking for her to come right inside, Gretta decided to speak. Something was going on, she couldn't read his mind, and at the moment she was tired of trying. "Joshua, what is it? What is wrong? And don't say nothin' because I know something is. You've usually had lots of things to say to me. Lately you've been as quiet as a winter hare."

"It has to do with the Allens," he said finally.

Gretta struggled to place them. Then, recalling the new English family who'd moved next door to them, she said, "Your new neighbors? What about them?"

"They have a daughter."

"Yes?" Surely their little girl wasn't being a pest? "What is wrong with that?"

"Nothing. It's just that." He sighed. "It's like this, Gretta. Lilly and I have struck a friendship."

"Lilly?"

"Yes. That's the daughter's name."

A sense of foreboding filled her. "How old is she?"

"I don't know. Seventeen? Eighteen? Our age. A little younger, maybe."

Our age? He was phrasing it like this Lilly was part of their group. But she wasn't. She could never be. "I don't understand why you are even thinking about her."

"To be honest, I don't know why either, except that I am. Lilly has made me think twice about the way things are with me. With us."

"How so? I don't understand how an *Englischer* has anything to do with you, or with us."

"You need to try. Seeing her has made me think about things."

"But why? This Lilly might be really nice, but she doesn't have all that much to do with us, and with our community, does she? She'll never be a person that we'll be close to."

He looked hurt by her words. "She might. Just because she's English doesn't mean we can't befriend her."

Now he was talking nonsense. Joshua Graber was a kind man, that was true. He also made friends easily, and had no problem selling to the English in their country store. But never before had he ever talked of being interested in their day-to-day business.

He'd never even mentioned his old neighbors the Wilsons in that way, and his family

81

had always enjoyed their company very much.

"Joshua, I'm trying to understand — I am. But I'm afraid I do not."

"I realize that," he said heavily, just as he halted Jim and pulled up the buggy's brake. "But getting to know her has got me thinking. About things in my life."

"Are you trying to tell me that you fancy her? In a courting way?" Even as she asked the words, every part of her insides were screaming. His pronouncement felt unfair to her. She was the one who'd always been around. Who had been waiting for the years to go by. Who was willing to do almost anything for him. Surely no *Englischer* could step in so easily and take that away?

Everyone knew she and Joshua were courting. Everyone was planning on them to be married within the next year or two. And though at times she, too, had had her doubts, she'd assumed the same things.

His expression looking far-off, he shrugged. "I don't know if I like her or not. But I do have to say that I've been thinking about her something fierce. Probably more than I should."

Those were not the words she'd been hoping to hear. Had ever expected to hear. "I don't know what to think."

"Maybe I should explain things . . ."

"I think not." She had no desire to hear him speak of another girl. To hear him admit that his heart had strayed.

"Joshua, I don't think we should discuss Lilly." She frowned. The unfamiliar name sounded choppy coming from her lips. Not smooth and flowing like when he said the girl's name.

He looked down. "All right. But Gretta, I have to tell ya something. Meeting Lilly has me worrying about us. About our future."

The things he was saying should have been breaking her heart. After all, she'd spent many a night dreaming about a life with him. Her parents had even let her spend some of the money she earned at the restaurant to buy things for her hope chest.

But now things were different. Now she recalled too well how distant he'd felt just sitting right next to her. She'd sensed that they'd been growing and changing and maybe wanted different things.

More than anything, she wanted a peaceful marriage. One without surprises, but with warmth and humor. Perhaps Joshua couldn't give her those things after all.

"See, what I'm trying to say is . . . if I can be thinking about Lilly . . . about an English girl. So quickly, so easily . . . maybe I'm not as ready for a serious relationship as I'd thought."

"I understand." Gretta quietly opened her door, stepped down, and stood, hardly noticing that snow had started to fall while they'd been riding home from the skating pond.

He blinked. "Do you? Because I surely don't know what's going on. All I know is that in the pit of my stomach things aren't like they used to be."

This was it. She could pretend ignorance, or give him honesty. "Sometimes I . . . I feel the same way. Sometimes I wonder if the Lord placed us together because He wants us together, as a married couple . . . or just to be friends."

"You've felt that way too sometimes? Really, Gretta?"

"Really." In spite of what she'd just said, Gretta wished he didn't sound quite so pleased. "I suppose we'll have to pray on this some."

"Yes. We should both do some praying. But for now, I think we need to stop our buggy rides and skating times together. At least for now."

She couldn't help but notice that he was more attentive now that she was not so moony over him. "I agree," she said simply.

It wasn't an easy thing to say, though. To say or to feel. For so long, Joshua Graber had been her dream for a bright future. But now, well, perhaps he was destined to merely be just a part of her past.

Searching her face, he replied slowly, "I'm glad you are being so understanding. It will all be for the best."

"I'm sure it will be." She turned then and walked away. Ran from any reply he might have, or before she lost her nerve.

Before she had to realize that she'd lost him.

As soon as the door closed, she leaned against it and breathed deep. *Lord Jesus,* she prayed. *Why is this happening? Why did you bring that Lilly into our community? Why did you make Joshua's attention stray?*

Help me. Help me know what to do, guide me, help me erase my fears.

Because at the moment, I feel so alone.

"Gretta, are you coming in?"

"*Jah,* Mamm," Gretta said, swiping her eyes. "I'm coming in right now."

"Is Joshua with you?"

"He is not. He, uh, he had other things to do today." Uneager to face her parents' questions, Gretta pulled off her cloak, hung it on the hook by the door, and stomped her feet good. "I'm going down to the basement to work on the laundry. I imagine the clothes on the lines are dry by now."

"*Danke,* Gretta. You'll make Joshua a fine wife one day."

"Yes, Mamm." Gretta gripped the rail tight as she headed down the stairs. What would her parents say if she told them what had just happened?

That everything they'd been counting on for her might not be, after all? She knew they'd be disappointed in her, and wonder how she could be so foolish.

As her eyes focused in the basement's dim light, Gretta realized that no matter what, she felt older and wiser.

And, unfortunately, saddened by what used to be . . . and by what may never be again.

CHAPTER 6

Lilly folded the letter she received from their former neighbor and placed it on the kitchen table with a sigh.

"What's that?" Charlie asked from the couch across the way.

"Oh, nothing. It's just a letter from Mrs. Casey."

"What did she want?"

"Nothing. Just to see how we were doing." Lilly wasn't sure what else to say. Lately, Charlie had been so surly, just about anything she said had the ability to set him off.

Pushing the textbook he was reading to one side, he joined her in the kitchen and read through the note, too. "I sure could go for one of her cookies right about now."

"She did make the best cookies," Lilly agreed. When she and Charlie were small, they used to be inseparable. Together, they'd run all over the neighborhood, going this way and that, making new friends and exploring the woods around their home. Mrs. Casey used to keep an eye on them when their mom was at work.

Still looking at the letter, Charlie said, "Did you see that she wants to come visit?"

"I did."

A frown worried his brow. "She doesn't know you're pregnant."

"I know." No one outside their family knew besides Alec and his family. And Ms. Vonn. "I don't know what Mom and Dad are going to say." Only half teasing, she said, "I guess they'll put her off or send me out of the house when she comes."

"They wouldn't do that, Lilly."

She patted her stomach. Most people would never have any idea that her tummy had grown. But anyone who knew her well — like Mrs. Casey — would instantly notice the differences in her body. "They might. Mom really doesn't want anyone to find out about the baby."

"She's trying to protect you."

"That's what Mom says, but sometimes I think it's for her benefit, too."

"Well, Mom's going to have to get used to your pregnancy soon. You're getting bigger, you know."

She chuckled. "Believe me, I know."

Sobering, she looked at her brother more closely. "Thanks for saying that about Mom, though. I thought you were mad at me."

He set the letter down and looked at her. "I was, but I was being stupid — it's not like you're the first girl in the world who's pregnant but not married." He shrugged. "Anyway, I'll be leaving soon. What's going on with you won't really be affecting my life in college."

"It won't at all."

He brightened. "Bowling Green next year is going to be great. And I'm starting to think that living here is going to be okay, too."

"Maybe." Looking in the direction of the Grabers, she smiled. "Our new neighbors aren't so bad."

"Maybe not. They're strange, but they're okay. That little guy, Anson, cracks me up."

She nodded. "He and Ty are becoming friends. At first I thought Dad was going to find something wrong with that, but I've caught him chatting with that kid a time or two."

Charlie rolled his eyes. "It would be impossible not to talk with Anson. He doesn't shut up."

"I would have guessed all the Amish to be like his brother, Joshua. Quiet, reserved.

Like they don't trust us *'Englischers.'*"

"Some don't act like they trust us. But some seem kind of different."

"You think so?"

"Yeah." After a moment, Charlie added, "I started talking to a girl the other day. She was outside the dry cleaners waiting for a ride when I finished working."

"What's she like?"

"She's Amish and pretty."

"What?" A few weeks ago, Lilly had wondered if Charlie would ever find any of the Amish girls pretty.

Looking sheepish, he rolled his eyes. "Yeah, I know. I was so sure I didn't want to make any friends here. No connections because I'm leaving."

"And because we have nothing in common with the Amish."

"I think I was wrong about that. Anyway, the girl, Mary, had a beagle."

"Really? Did he look like Britches?" Their old beagle had been part of the family until his death the year before.

"He looked almost exactly like him, he had the same markings and everything. At first I was just talking to Mary about that. Then we started talking about other stuff, too. She was nice."

"I wish Mom and Dad would give the

community a chance."

"Me too." At the moment, though, nothing with her parents seemed settled. All they did was talk about Ms. Vonn and Lilly's bright future. How no one would ever have to know that she'd given a baby up for adoption.

"Hey, Lilly? You don't . . . you don't feel like you're all alone, do you? I mean, you know you can always talk to me, right?"

She'd used to think that. She used to depend on that. Lately, though, she'd thought that was all in their past. She couldn't have been happier to hear his words. "I didn't think I could . . . but now I will."

He squeezed her shoulders before heading toward the stairs.

"Hey, Charlie?"

"Yeah?"

"If Mrs. Casey comes . . ." her voice drifted off, unsure of how to put her fears into the right words.

It turned out, she didn't have to. "If Mrs. Casey comes for a visit, I'll make sure Mom doesn't hide you. Mrs. Casey is just going to have to find out the truth about you."

"And if she's shocked?"

He waved a hand. "If she's shocked, she'll get over it." Smiling crookedly, he caught her eye. "I mean, I did."

For the first time in days, Lilly laughed. Maybe things were going to be okay, after all.

Hands sticky with dough, Gretta tried to blow a strand of hair away from her forehead, but the wisp of air didn't do any good. Her forehead was a bit damp from kneading the large amount of dough by herself. With a sigh, Gretta resigned herself to having hair in her eyes for a few moments longer.

She had no choice in the matter, anyway. Miriam had taken the day off to help her mother with the cleaning since they were hosting church on Sunday. Kelly, an *Englischer* who sometimes came in to help with soups and main dishes, had called in sick.

It was up to Gretta to make all the cinnamon rolls by herself.

Usually, she enjoyed the time-consuming project very much. However, today she only looked at the rising dough and wished things would happen a little faster. The snow was coming down fast.

When the front door opened and shut, Mrs. Kent poked her head out from the back room. "Can you help them, Gretta?

I've got my hands full, sorting bills this morning."

Though she wasn't at her best with customers — Gretta knew she was too shy for that — she did, every now and then, enjoy getting out from behind the wide wooden worktable. A fair portion of their customers were Amish. Visiting with them while she took their orders was a good way to catch up on the community chitchat.

"I'll be right out, Mrs. Kent." After hastily covering the dough with a clean cloth, she washed off the sticky dough from her hands, wiped her brow, and smoothed her hair back in place. Only then was she able to walk through the swinging doors to the twelve-table dining area.

But when she saw who'd walked in the door, her feet stilled like they were frozen in the skating pond. "Roland?"

A slow, playful smile lit his face as he took notice of her surprise. "Hi, there, Gretta," he said as he practically sauntered toward her.

Her feet still glued to the ground, Gretta felt as if her skin was burning from the tips of her ears to the ends of her toes when he stopped directly in front of her. "Why are you here?"

His eyes widened. "For coffee, of course."

93

"Oh, yes. Yes, of course." If she could have run away, she would have, she was so embarrassed. Of course he'd be coming to the restaurant for food or drink! Why else would he have come?

Feeling mighty flustered, her voice turned sharp. "Go take a table if you would like."

But instead of walking to one of the tables she pointed to, he bypassed them all and took one of the six bar stools at the counter. "I'd rather sit here, I think."

Once he got settled, she walked behind the counter and picked up a little notepad the waitresses used. "So, you'd like some coffee?"

"I would." Lines formed around his eyes as he watched her fumble with the stub of a pencil she'd picked up, too.

Now she felt even more foolish. He was obviously waiting to see if she needed to write that order down! Well, there was only one thing to do. She slapped the notepad on the counter and tried to act like she catered to customers all the time. "I'll get that right out for you."

"I did want the coffee, but I really came in to see if you were needin' a ride home later on today."

She paused on her way to the coffeepot. "A ride?"

"Yes." Looking almost bashful — though that would be quite a feat for Roland, for he was never shy — he said, "It's terribly cold out, and the snow's already started to fall. I'd hate for you to have to walk home in that."

She only lived six blocks from the restaurant. It was one of the reasons her parents had allowed her to work at the Sugarcreek Inn. Walking six blocks in the snow would not be a hardship at all. "That's a kind offer, but I don't think I'll be needing it." Grabbing a thick white mug, she poured the dark brew all the way to the rim, only realizing after she was done that she didn't know if he enjoyed milk in his coffee.

Joshua always took cream and sugar.

When she placed the mug in front of him, Roland clasped his hands around the base, warming his fingers. "It's not just a kind offer. I heard some news about you."

"Me?"

"Well, news about you and Joshua Graber."

"Do you plan to share it?" She was so caught off-guard, Gretta half hoped her high and mighty tone would set him off and prevent him from saying another word about her and Joshua.

But it wasn't to be. "I heard that you and

95

Joshua weren't so particular about each other anymore."

Well, so the rumor mill had already begun spinning! Gretta struggled to hide her feelings. It was hard to hear that she was the subject of gossip. Harder still to know that the gossip held some truth.

"It's a shame that people gossip like they do," she murmured, just as a tear threatened to fall. She turned away again and pulled off a container of sugar and poured a small amount of cream into a heavy blue pitcher the size of her fist. After taking a moment to compose herself, she set the pair in front of him.

But Roland made no move to reach for either. Instead, he kept gazing at her with cow eyes.

"Would you like a donut?"

"Sure." Looking far too relaxed and at ease all the sudden, Roland pointed to one of Miriam's chocolate-cake donuts that she'd made the night before. "I'll take that one there."

After she'd placed his request on a plate in front of him, he smiled. "So . . . will you let me give you a ride this afternoon, Gretta?"

"I'm not sure if it would be a *gut* idea."

"Why not?"

96

"People might talk . . ."

"Let them talk!" Puffing his chest a bit, Roland said, "I hope everyone we know sees me driving you home."

She most certainly did not want that. She'd be bombarded with all kinds of nosey questions.

"Come now, Gretta. Don't be so skittish. No matter what is going on between you and Joshua, you're still allowed to look around, don'tcha think?"

He did have a point. "Yes."

"Then?"

Then she knew the right thing to do was to step forward with a little jump. More than anything she wanted to be a wife and mother. An Amish wife and mother. That meant she needed to find a man in her community who she could get along with.

If Joshua didn't want her, perhaps she'd be just as happy with Roland. Happier even.

Maybe she should be giving him a chance — he seemed to be the kind of person who was dependable and patient. Those were wonderful-good attributes, and ones she would value.

After all, her place would be in the home. She'd need to tend to it, and be taking care of their future *kinner,* too. Roland would be working hard on his farm, taking care of his pigs and chickens, and the vegetable stand his family owned.

Maybe the Lord and Margaret and Josh and Roland were all trying to tell her the same thing — that she needed to look forward to practical dreams and desires. Not hugs and kisses and constant companionship.

Maybe it was past time she grew up.

"Yes, Roland, I'd be most grateful if you took me home today. I finish work at four."

Swiping his donut from the plate, Roland grinned. "I know. I already checked your schedule before I asked." And with that, he chomped down on the chocolate treat with one hand and poured a liberal amount of cream in his coffee with the other — never noticing just how full the mug was.

With a frown, Gretta watched a bit of liquid slid over the side and down onto the counter.

Roland didn't seem to mind. In fact, he was so pleased, he looked like he'd just sold one of his lambs for a mighty good price at an auction.

As she stood near him, she tried to smile, too. It was time to have a more open mind toward love and companionship. It was time to find happiness . . . any way that she could.

CHAPTER 7

At five o'clock, the snow fell thick outside the Graber Country Store's front window. Already Sugarcreek had received six inches. Joshua had heard from a few English customers that more was on the way, as well as a temperature drop. One man had stated that this month was on track to be the coldest January in ten years.

All Joshua knew was that it was going to take him twice as long as usual to get home, and Jim wouldn't care for the snowy roads either.

Few people were in the store. As the wind picked up outside, swirling the falling snow every which way, his father worriedly looked at the large clock decorating the store's entrance almost every five minutes. "We should probably close for the day, but we're still due to get a load from the dairy in Berlin."

"Maybe they'll postpone the trip?" Joshua

ventured. But even as he asked, he knew it was a foolish question. Milk needed to be delivered when it was fresh. Always.

"I don't think so. Plus the weather's most likely not too bad for that big truck."

When he noticed his father watching the snow with a frown a few moments later, Joshua patted his shoulder. "I'll wait for it, Daed. You take Judith and head toward home."

"But how will you get home?"

"If it's bad, I'll spend the night. If it's not so bad I'll walk."

"It's a long four miles in the snow. I know, I've walked it myself."

"That's why it's my turn, yes?" Joshua shrugged. "Perhaps I'll see someone I know and he'll give me a ride. But Jim won't care for the roads if the snow gets much deeper. It's time for you to go on."

"Can we do that, Daed?" Judith asked, her eyes shining with hope. "There's no one here. I just rang the last customer up."

"I suppose we can, then." Turning toward Joshua, he added, "That is, if you are sure you don't mind, Joshua."

"I don't. Go on now."

"I guess we will. Get your things together, Judith, then get the basket full of items your mother asked for this morning. I'll go break the news to Jim that he's gonna have to leave his cozy stable in the back."

Joshua grinned as his sister instantly strode off to retrieve their mother's requests. "Judith's anxious to be on her way."

"She's always anxious to be on her way," his father agreed with a laugh. "All right, then. Joshua, if I don't see you in three hours, I'm gonna be hoping you are staying here."

"I'll stay here until the delivery truck comes, then be on my way," Joshua promised.

Moments later, Joshua watched their familiar black buggy make its way down the side street and head toward home, the lantern hanging in the back window casting an orange glow through the multitude of flakes.

As the wheels made thin lines in the street, Joshua smiled.

In truth, he'd been exaggerating a bit about his fears for their trusty horse. Joshua didn't think Jim was finding the snow to be a problem at all — he'd just wanted to lessen his father's worries. If Daed had stayed at the store, he would have felt torn, worrying about Mamm and the little ones at home.

Joshua was now old enough to take over a

lot of the store's responsibilities, even if his father didn't always realize it.

Feeling somewhat like his father, he glanced at the clock again. Five thirty. The truck should be along momentarily.

He decided to dust off the back ledge and straighten the area where baskets and wooden toys were. A group of children had come in an hour before and had not been shy about playing with the wooden trains and stable animals.

He'd just picked up a pair of delicately carved sheep when the bell rang.

"I was wonderin' if ya were gonna be able to get here today, Ben . . ."

But it wasn't Ben who greeted him with a smile. No, it was his neighbor. Lilly.

"Hi. I, um, I'm not Ben."

No, she surely wasn't. "I'm expecting a delivery truck," he explained, not certain if his statement was much of an explanation at all.

"Oh, it's here, too." She gestured over her shoulder. "He pulled up just as Charlie was parking."

The door flew open again, spraying the display of baskets with a dusting of snow. And in walked Ben, his solid muscular arms loaded down with supplies as usual. "Joshua! Good evening! I've got a full load of milk, butter, and cream for you today. There're boxes in the back of books and leather goods, too."

"I'll pull on my gloves and help you." Belatedly, Joshua looked Lilly's way. "Unless there's something you were needin' first?"

Looking bemused, she shook her head. "No. I mean, I have time. Charlie's on his way in, too."

"All right, then."

Sure enough, in came Charlie just as Joshua slipped on his gloves and followed Ben outside. "Do you need any help with that?" Charlie asked.

"No. It's my job, not yours. You go on in out from the cold."

After Charlie disappeared through the door with another clink of bells, Joshua clambered inside the truck's spacious bed and pulled out a wooden crate.

Its weight momentarily took his breath away before he steadied himself. "I always forget how heavy these trays of milk are," he grumbled to Ben as he followed Ben's footsteps on the snowy walkway.

"Don't worry, you'll be remembering soon enough," the burly thirty-year-old said with a grin.

Five turns later, Joshua was signing the

103

receipt and waving Ben on his way.

He slipped in the back door and hastily went to the wash room and wiped off his brow. Even in the snowy weather, he'd managed to work up a sweat.

After that, he looked for Lilly and Charlie, and found them next to the baked goods. "Are you needin' some bread or rolls?"

Lilly nodded. "We do. And some fresh cheese and yogurt too, if you have it."

Charlie stood to one side while Joshua retrieved the items for her. "Anything else?"

"No, this is it." Looking at her brother, she nibbled on her bottom lip a bit uncertainly. "We've got to get on home. The streets are really getting bad. Since the storm came up so quickly, I don't know if the salt trucks have been out yet."

"I best be letting ya get on your way, then." Carefully, he punched in each item on the cash register. "Eighteen dollars and seventy-six cents."

She handed him a twenty. "When will you leave?"

"Soon. You two are my last customers."

When Charlie joined them at the counter he whistled low. "I've never seen your store so quiet. Where's everyone else?"

"The snow scared the rest of the customers away, I'm thinking."

Lilly waved a hand. "Your family, too?"

"I sent my *daed* and sister on home. The roads were getting icy. I didn't want to worry about Jim slipping."

Charlie tilted his head. "Jim?"

"He's our —"

"Horse," Lilly finished with a smile. "I met him the day Mom sent over that cake."

Joshua handed Lilly her sack. "Well, here's your things. Thank you for comin' in."

"Thank you." Turning to her brother, Lilly wrapped her gray wool muffler around her neck. "Charlie? You ready?"

"Yeah, sure." Charlie pushed off from the wall, then took the sack from Lilly. "Hey, Josh, if your horse and buggy is gone, how are you getting home?"

"I'll be walking."

Lilly's eyes widened. "It's quite a ways."

"It is," Joshua agreed. "But I'll be fine. I've walked farther in worse weather before."

"We can give you a ride, if you want," Charlie blurted. "That is, if you ever ride in cars and trucks."

"We do. We can ride in vehicles, just not own them."

"Well, you want a ride with us? It's no trouble."

105

Joshua made a sudden decision though there really wasn't much of a choice to make. He could either spend the next hour or so walking through snow or ride home in the truck's relative comfort. "*Danke.* I'd be mighty grateful. I just have to go lock up."

Lilly smiled at her brother. "No hurry. Take your time."

Lilly was aware of every single move that Joshua Graber made. From the contemplative way he studied them, to the easy movement of his body, lifting those heavy packages from the truck without much more than a small grimace.

She caught him smiling in appreciation when they climbed in the cab of Charlie's black truck, taking a moment to run a finger over the hood before getting in on the other side of her.

When he noticed that she noticed, his cheeks reddened. "I was just thinkin' about how much my brother Caleb would like to be in my shoes. He likes this truck very much."

Before Lilly could say anything, Charlie spoke up. "Hey, anytime he wants a ride, just let me know. I'll give him one."

"I'll tell Caleb. That will make him happy, indeed."

"Good."

Lilly turned to her brother in surprise. What was going on with him? Usually he never put himself out for anyone. And, last she'd heard, he hadn't been in any hurry to be friends with their Amish neighbors either. Was he trying to make friends . . . or simply just trying to do the right thing?

They bumped along the snowy road that had been recently salted. With each mile gained, the group of stores behind them began to fade behind the thick curtain of snow.

Joshua seemed content to ride in silence, merely looking out the window. For his part, Charlie seemed relaxed, too. Usually he blared his music or complained about something. Now, though, whether it was because of the poor road conditions or Joshua's presence, he drove without saying much.

As they turned a corner and entered Old Ranch Trail, the broad street which both their homes branched off of, Lilly decided to speak. She was too curious about Josh to pass up the opportunity to learn more about him. "So I guess your family has lived here a long time."

"Oh, yes. Four generations now."

"And you've always had the store?"

"No. We were farmers for most of that time. Things changed when farmland got expensive, though. My grandfather was always a master planner, and terribly shrewd, too. He started thinking that maybe our community didn't need another set of struggling farmers as much as a store to see to our needs. Until we built this store, most folks had to drive to Berlin to get most of their necessities."

"And so you built that big building?" Lilly asked.

"Oh, no. My grandfather built a smallish building at first. When business got good, he added on. My father added on, too."

Charlie turned Joshua's way. "So . . . do you like working there?"

"Well enough. It's all I've known, and it's what's been expected of me." Looking over Lilly to Charlie, Joshua said, "I hear you go to college."

"Yep. Well, I was in college before we moved. I'm working over at the dry cleaners in order to save up some money to pay for room and board."

"He wants to live in the dorm at Bowling Green," Lilly added, thinking she was both literally and figuratively in the middle of the conversation.

Drumming his hand on the steering wheel,

Charlie nodded. "I went to a community college this fall, but had to stop when we moved here."

"Now that's a shame."

Though Joshua didn't say anything more, Lilly felt awkward. She didn't like being reminded about how she was the reason for Charlie's college break and she really didn't want her brother mentioning her pregnancy.

"Next fall Charlie will be off at college again," she said quickly.

"And you?"

Now that was the hundred-dollar question! She sure didn't know what she wanted to do. "I'm not sure what I'll be doing in the fall."

"Ah."

Thankfully, for once Charlie didn't add his feelings about the whole subject. Instead he said nothing, just continued driving.

After a moment, Joshua looked at her again. "What else would you do besides go to college? You want to work? Do you have a sweetheart?"

Charlie scoffed under his breath.

Lilly attempted not to smile at Josh's quaint phrase. "A sweetheart? Um, no I don't. Well, I don't anymore."

Looking increasingly interested, Josh continued to gaze at her. "But you did?"

"Yeah. I guess I did. He's back in Cleveland, though. And we're over."

"Why?"

She wanted to chide him for being so nosey, but she didn't feel as if she could. After all, she was the one who'd pushed for conversation. She was the one who'd brought up Alec, too.

And, as she looked into his eyes, Lilly realized Josh wasn't being all that prying at all. More like . . . direct. Actually, it just seemed like asking those kinds of questions were commonplace for him.

Lilly recalled how her mom said she'd learned that most Amish didn't speak in meaningless half-truths. They asked meaningful questions and expected direct answers.

Well, she could go with that. "Things happened. We, um, decided to have different futures."

"You don't think you could have worked things out?"

"No."

"Did neither of you want to?"

Now she felt tongue-tied. Josh was forcing her to say out loud all of the confusing feelings she'd been experiencing for the last four months.

She didn't know if she could.

110

"We're here," Charlie said abruptly. "I think it would be best if you got right out so we could get home, too."

"Oh. Yes. Thank you for the ride," he murmured as he climbed out of the cab. "It would have been a long walk home."

Because Charlie didn't say a word, Lilly smiled enough for both of them. "You're welcome, Josh."

As soon as Josh turned away Charlie pulled the truck into gear and made his way down the Grabers' driveway. Rocks crunched under the wheels as he exited.

"That guy's such a piece of work. Here I was, trying to do the right thing and give him a ride home and he repaid us by asking a dozen questions."

"I don't think he was being rude. We asked him questions, too."

"His were a lot more personal," Charlie said as he turned left out of the Grabers' driveway then almost immediately turned into their own yard.

"They weren't that bad."

After placing the truck in park, Charlie turned to her. "Bad enough. Lilly, he's probably got his eye on you."

"I doubt that. I bet he already has a girlfriend, anyway."

As Charlie opened his door and hopped

out of the cab onto a cushion of packed snow, he said, "I sure hope he does. I hope he's got a great girlfriend who he's in love with. Because the last thing you need, Lilly, is to be involved with another guy."

Curving her arms protectively around her stomach, Lilly said, "Don't worry. I won't be. Not any time soon."

But she sure wouldn't mind a friend. That, she could use. Of course Lilly had an idea that a guy like Joshua Graber would never be friends with a girl who got pregnant out of wedlock. No, if he knew the truth about her, why, he probably would never have said a word to her.

Picking up the grocery sack that Charlie had forgotten, she slowly made her way into the house, being careful not to slip on a patch of ice. How much her life had changed. Sometimes she couldn't help but long for the days when she was just plain old Lilly Allen, no secrets to shame her.

CHAPTER 8

The afternoon before, Gretta had done her best to brush aside the questions her mother tossed her way about why Roland had brought her home. It had almost been easy because things were so out of sorts at their house.

Margaret was home with a fever. Because of that, their mother had left the quilt shop early in order to tend to her needs. But her mother still had sewing to do. She'd promised a customer that she'd piece together a miniature star quilt by the next day.

As soon as Gretta walked inside, she'd been asked to make dinner. All afternoon her mother had been running back and forth from Margaret's room to the kitchen table, doing her best to tend to Margaret and piece together the bright yellow, orange, blue, and red triangles of cloth.

To help out, Gretta had made chicken and dumplings, served it to her parents when it was ready, then washed all the dishes and wiped down the table while her mother went back to her project and her father went outside to shovel snow.

Later, she'd had to attend to her usual chore of laundry.

All the activity had been a blessing. Her mother had been too busy taking care of her sister and sewing to do much more than ask Gretta a few questions about Joshua's sudden absence from their door. Gretta had been able to produce a few vague answers to the whole question of Roland.

Today she wasn't faring so well. Margaret was back at school, her father was at work, and neither she nor her mother had work scheduled. They'd been alone together for most of the day.

It had felt endless.

"So why is it again that Roland came to be dropping you home, Gretta? I still don't understand why he offered such a thing," her mother asked as together they oiled the kitchen cabinets with thick rags.

Though they'd already discussed this, and Gretta was feeling frustrated with her mother's constant questioning, Gretta took care to keep her voice slow and even. "He came to the restaurant and asked," she said simply. "Since it was snowing, I accepted."

"You make this development sound easy and spontaneous, but I'm afraid it's not. This Roland coming by means something, I fear."

"I don't think it's something to fear, Mamm. It was only a buggy ride home."

"Maybe. Maybe not." After dabbing another amount of oil on her cloth, her *mamm* leveled another probing glance her way. "Now, tell me about Joshua. Why hasn't he come calling?"

"He took me skating two weeks ago."

"But nothing since. That's not like him." She rubbed hard at a scuff mark on the bottom of a cabinet. "What happened, do you think?"

Well, that was an easy thing to tell the truth about — even if it was embarrassing. "I don't know."

"I think you do. Please talk to me, daughter."

Oh, her mother had an iron will! Gretta felt like she could no more escape her mother's questions than she could leave the house with her hair down around her back. "I don't know what to say."

"Gretta, until recently, things were much different between you and Joshua. He was attentive and you seemed happier. Now you seem sad and Joshua hasn't stopped by.

Most certainly nothing is going right. What has happened?"

"Things . . . things have changed between us."

"Changed? How? What did you do?"

Gretta closed her eyes, miserable. In her heart, she knew that her mother didn't mean to sound so harsh, so judgmental. But that's how her words felt. "I didn't do anything."

"Were you not respectful and thoughtful?"

"I was."

She paused. "Perhaps you haven't spent enough time with his family. An Amish man likes to know that his wife will get along well with his family."

Honestly, her mother was acting as if the Grabers were practically strangers, not folks who they'd known all their lives. "I don't think our differences had anything to do with my lack of time with his family."

With a little moan, her mother stood straight and rubbed her back. "Bending over to polish the wood seems to get harder every year." After she massaged the small of her back, her mother brightened. "I know! Perhaps you could make him a pie. We know how Joshua does have a sweet tooth."

Remembering how strained their conversation had been the last time he'd come over, Gretta shook her head. "Pie won't help."

"Then what will? You need to do something to get back Joshua's regard."

"He wants to take a break, and only time will help with that." Desperate to move the subject to something more positive, Gretta said, "Why are you upset with Roland bringing me home, anyway? Do you not think much of Roland? I thought you enjoyed his mother's company."

Outside the kitchen door, Gretta heard her father's low, musical voice as he talked to Stormy, their horse. In no time, he'd be walking into the house.

For a moment, Gretta glanced her mother's way, sure and hopeful that she'd leave their discussion for another time and go see to her husband's needs.

But this time, she did not. This time, she kept talking, just as if Gretta wasn't miserable enough and if her father wasn't just on the other side of the door.

"His mother is a *gut* friend, that is true. But I don't think he is your chosen man. Tell me what you and Joshua have been talking about. We need to decide what went wrong and what you can do to catch his attention."

Oh, but her mother would have made a

terribly good police officer . . . she certainly knew how to obtain a confession! Already exhausted with the questions, trying to keep her mother at arm's length, Gretta gave in. "We talked the other day and decided that perhaps we'd been too hasty with our courting."

"Too hasty? You've known him for years. That doesn't make a bit of sense to me."

"I know it doesn't." Oh, but her mother never knew when to be quiet. She'd never seen the need to keep her opinions to herself. It was both a pleasing quality of hers and a frustrating one. Gretta had a feeling her father had felt frustrated quite often, too.

"Daughter, explain things now."

"There's nothing to explain to you," Gretta snapped, her patience at an end. "I know you want me to be happy with Joshua, but he and I may not be happy together, after all."

"Then you should —"

"No. Don't tell me what you think I should do about Joshua and me. It is not any of your concern."

Face florid, her mother stood up just as her father entered the room, his expression alarmed. "Of course it is," her mother said matter-of-factly. "You're my daughter. I have every right to know what you and Joshua say to each other."

"No, you don't. It's my life. I have a right to make my way. I have a right to make decisions about it."

"Not if you make a mess of it."

"You can't know that is what I'm doing."

True anger flashed in mother's eyes. "I've never been more disappointed in you, Gretta. I promise, if you continue with that disrespectful tone —"

Her father finally entered the argument. "Katherine, you must stop this now."

Shock flew in waves as his words reverberated through the room. Never before had she heard her father speak that way to her mother. Never before had he interfered with one of mother's lectures.

Face slack, she turned to her husband. "Ben?"

His voice softer, but no less stern, he said, "I've heard enough of your speaking so harshly to our Gretta." After a pause he added, "Perhaps you should go collect yourself."

Though her mother said nothing more, her displeasure was evident in every step out of the room.

Gretta held her breath as her father took one of the kitchen chairs, gesturing for her to take one, too. When she obediently sat, she waited expectantly. What was he going to say? Would he, too, chide her for not procuring Joshua's marriage proposal?

"I heard much of what your mother and you said," he finally murmured after examining her for a good long moment. "Your mother and I want the same thing, daughter. We both want you to be happy."

"I don't think so."

"I'm tellin' the truth, I promise."

"Daed, you heard what she said."

"I did." His eyes so patient and kind, he continued. "She thinks you and Joshua are meant to be together, that's all."

"What do you think?" she asked slowly.

"I just want you to be happy. That's all." Ever so slowly, he held his arms to her.

Almost as slowly, she stepped forward and hugged him. Oh, but her *daed* was so solid, and so strong. Always his arms had felt stronger than anyone else's. Always he'd seemed taller and better than anyone else.

Though he and her mother had had their share of troubles, she still needed his support. Tears escaped and fell to his shirt as she closed her eyes and let herself just feel. And be loved. "I'm sorry," she said, though she wasn't sure what she was sorry for . . . *the words to her mother? The fact that Joshua*

120

wanted more time?

The fact that she wasn't — and never could be — as good as her sister Beth?

"I'm sorry I didn't mind my tongue better."

"It will be all right, daughter," he murmured. "You'll see. Our Lord God works in mysterious ways, there's no doubt of that. One day we'll wake up and realize everything has been taken care of."

Gretta did believe that the Lord would help her, but she also feared she'd not been understanding some of the things He'd been wanting her to.

All her plans felt hard to catch, like they were flying away, and too small and fragile to grab ahold of. "But I don't know what to do, Daed."

After another squeeze, he stepped back from her and, like when she was a child, ran one rough finger under her eye, taking her tears with it. *"Sur gut, jah?"*

Instead of feeling reassured, she only felt more confused by his words. "Why is it good?"

"Because only our Lord knows what to do. We just have to listen."

Warily, she looked toward the basement door, where she heard her mother bustling about doing the laundry. Oh, but her mother was in a state. When the loud thud of water hitting the wash bin wafted up the stairs, she bit her lip. "I don't know what to say to Mamm."

To Gretta's surprise, instead of looking angry her father chuckled. "She's in a temper, but she'll calm down soon enough." He waved a hand. "Go on, now. You tell her that you'll help with dinner, just like always. That's enough."

Feeling like she was on her way to the gallows, Gretta stepped toward the staircase and did as she was bid. No, she didn't know what things the future had in store for her.

But she did know some things. No matter what tomorrow brought, today she needed to be a good daughter. And that involved saying she was sorry to her mother and asking how she could help.

It was what was expected of a good Amish daughter. And that was something she would always try to be.

"So, Joshua, perhaps you could talk to us all about your new friendship with the *Englischer* next door." Elsa Graber announced at dinner on Thursday evening. "It seems to me that perhaps there is more to your friendship with the girl than I realized."

In unison, all seven of the kids set their

knives and forks down. At the head of the wide oak table, their father paused in mid-chew. Though their mother's tone and language was calm, there was an unmistakable note of force in it. She most certainly did not bring up the topic by chance. She wanted some information, and wanted it sooner than later.

Peeking to his right, Josh caught Caleb's eye. Perhaps something had occurred to bring such an announcement on that he didn't know about. Maybe Caleb had stayed out too late the evening before? His brother was surely enjoying his *rumspringa*. Sometimes a mite too much, Joshua felt.

But if Caleb knew, he wasn't telling. He simply looked right back at him and shrugged.

After another moment of surprised silence, their father spoke. "What is worrying you, Elsa?"

Carefully arranging her silverware on her plate, she shrugged. "I'm not worried . . . I'm merely interested in Joshua's life. There's nothing wrong with that."

While Judith coughed into her napkin, Carrie, Anson, and Caleb studiously began eating again. Everyone knew from experience that once their mother was determined to find out something, nothing was going to sway her.

"What did you want to know about me and Lilly, Mamm?"

For a moment, she looked taken aback by his direct question. Then she sat up a bit straighter. "For one thing, I'm curious as to why you're going riding around with Lilly and her brother now."

"It was snowing outside, Mamm. The only reason I got home at all was because Charlie and Lilly Allen gave me a ride." Unbidden, he felt his cheeks heat up. He was starting to feel like Anson. All of nine and under constant surveillance.

"It was snowing something awful," Judith agreed. "It took Daed and I twice as long as usual to get here."

"I bet it was mighty nice, riding in a truck like that." Caleb shook his head in regret. "I knew I should've stayed longer at the store. Then I could've ridden with the Allens in the truck."

"I had a feeling you were gonna say that," Joshua said. "Charlie mentioned he'd be happy to take you for a ride whenever you wanted one."

Pure glee entered his brother's features. "I'll be wantin' one soon."

Farther down the long bench, Anson piped up. "I want to see it, too."

Caleb rolled his eyes. "Well, we know that ain't gonna happen. You're way too small."

"It might. I'm friends with Ty Allen. I am."

"I'm sure you are but that don't mean much," Caleb chided.

Deliberately, their mother cleared her throat. "I don't think we need to worry about the Allens' truck anymore. It's not likely any of you will be going for rides in it."

"Why not?" Caleb asked. "We went in the Wilsons' car from time to time."

"It was different, accepting rides from the Wilsons. They did not have children your age."

"But I like Ty," whined Anson. "What's wrong with him, Mamm?"

"Not a thing. It's just that they're English."

"I know that." Pushing his plate away, Anson looked like he might cry. "I know Ty's English. But I still like him."

"I know you do. And I'm glad you and Ty Allen get along, but we mustn't become too close," their mother warned. Measuring each of them a stern look, she added, "We just have to be careful that we don't let our feelings run out of control."

Josh had had enough. Impatiently, he swung his gaze to the opposite end of the table, to where their father had been carefully eating his canned peas. "Daed, what is the problem with the Allens?"

After a moment's reflection, his father answered. "Your mother —"

"Frank!"

Their father blushed. "I mean to say, we don't want you getting too tempted by their ways."

Caleb frowned. "By what ways? By their English clothes?"

"By everything. It's mainly you teenagers I've been thinking of," their mother said, looking hard at Joshua, Judith, and Caleb. "It's my duty to keep a close eye on you."

"I'm a bit old for that, don'tcha think?" Joshua asked.

"I would think so, but you've sure been taking your time about joining the church."

That statement made him uncomfortable. "I said I'd get baptized soon."

"But you'll never say when." His mother's chin went up. "Until you do, I don't think you should be doing things with the English, Joshua."

"I wasn't doing things with them. I was accepting a ride home. If I hadn't, I would have walked home in the snow. Is that what you wanted?"

"It is a blessing that Charlie drove you in

his truck. But what if accepting such things leads to something more?"

"Such as?"

Her chin went up. "Such as thinking about the outside world."

"Mamm —"

"Joshua, I heard you told Gretta that you wouldn't be seeing her for a while."

"Who told you that?" He turned to his sister. "Judith, was it you?"

"No it was not."

Elsa glared at Judith. "But you knew."

"Yes."

"What did she say to that?" Caleb wanted to know. "Did she cry?"

The dinner was getting more uncomfortable by the moment. Joshua tried to stem the flow of words. "Mamm, I canna believe that we are discussing such things. And at the table, too. Me and Gretta is nobody's business but our own."

Judith rolled her eyes. "That's like sayin' the sky only belongs to the person standing underneath it! Your business is our business, brother. And even if it wasn't, why we'd make it our own." Without stopping for breath, she leaned forward. "Now, then. What is wrong with you and Gretta?"

"Nothing."

"I think there is. Gretta's kin are saying

127

there is quite a bit wrong with the two of you. They're saying you are no longer calling on her."

"That is true."

"I wish you would have let your mother know that," his father said.

"Fine. If you all want to know everything, I will share it all with you. A few weeks ago, I asked Gretta for some time to think about things before we got more serious."

"You've known her for years, son." His father scrunched up his face. "For what do you need more time?"

"Time to think about things, that's what." In spite of himself, Joshua looked around the table at everyone and hoped his words would be understood. And that some advice would be given. "I've been restless. Feeling like I've had no say in my life."

"Our Lord God has been directing your life," Judith said. "You don't need a say in it."

Joshua was just about to find fault with that statement when he noticed his parents exchange amused glances. Ah, perhaps they weren't quite as unaware of his struggles as he'd imagined.

"Your mother and I just want you to have a care for Gretta's feelings," his daed murmured. "It's not her fault that you've grown restless."

"I know that."

After a moment, his mother smiled softly. "I am glad we talked about this. I know I, for one, am now feeling better." With a scrape of the chair, his mother stood up. "Now then, I made a shoo-fly pie this morning. Who would care for a slice with some coffee?"

The little ones clapped in excitement. Even Caleb and Anson grinned. Quietly, Judith stood up to help. As she always did.

Joshua truly did appreciate their customs. He did. He couldn't imagine not living the way his ancestors always had before him.

He just wanted some time to think on it. Closing his eyes, he silently gave thanks for the reprieve.

CHAPTER 9

Lilly didn't know what to do when her dad got out the adoption book again while they were eating breakfast. No matter what time of day it was, thoughts about her future always seemed to make it into the conversation.

"You need to choose a family to take the baby, Lilly," he said. "We can't put this off much longer. People are waiting and trying to plan their lives."

She stared at the plain cover of the loosely bound notebook. "I know that."

Opening the book almost reverently, his voice softened as he flipped through the pages. "The other night when I couldn't sleep I read through the whole thing. There are some really good people on these pages, Lilly. Their stories about trying to conceive are heartbreaking, and the steps they've taken to ensure that you will be treated with respect and gratitude is commendable.

Please make a decision, or at the very least, narrow down your choices like we've asked you to."

Lilly had read all the pages, too. She'd read every couple's bio and looked at the pictures of their homes, their yards, even their pet dogs. But instead of being inspired, all she'd felt was a thick knot of dread forming in her stomach.

She didn't know whether her anxiety came from having to make such an important choice, from knowing she was going to disappoint so many people . . . or from her most private reason of all. "It's hard to choose, Dad."

"I know, but it has to be done." With a gentle smile, he said, "Lillian, I really think you'll feel better once a decision has been made."

He was right. There was so much tension in their family, things could only get better when she made a choice.

And, well, she had . . . but it wasn't the choice her parents had ever wanted to consider. Slowly, she ventured, "Maybe I should just keep the baby."

With a look of regret, he closed the book's cover. "There's more to keeping the baby than simply holding a sweet newborn. It's a commitment of a lifetime."

"I can be committed."

"I know you can, honey. But please think about your future. Think about all the things you used to dream about doing. You won't be able to fulfill those dreams with a baby in tow."

When her dad said things like that, Lilly always wondered what her father had missed out on. What dreams did he have that were unfulfilled?

When the silence spread thick between them, he tapped the table. "Hey, remember when you wanted to fly planes?"

"I remember." That had been a childish whim when she'd been twelve. For her dad to bring it up when she was trying to have a real, meaningful conversation with him felt like a slap in the face. "That was a long time ago, you know."

"But it's still a possibility. Right now, everything you've always wanted to do could happen. If you have a baby to take care of, though, things will change. You won't be able to do half as much."

"You and Mom always say you never regret having kids."

"That's different, and you know it."

"Not really."

"Lilly, your mother and I got married first. You are not married."

"I know."

"In addition, Mom and I planned to be together for the rest of our lives. We planned for children, too."

"But you didn't plan for Ty. Mom said he was a surprise."

A flicker of pain crossed his face. "Ty was a surprise because your mother had two miscarriages. We didn't think we could have any more children after you."

The news made her dizzy. Somehow, learning that her parents had gone through monumental crises while she'd been oblivious to them made her uncomfortable. "I . . . I didn't know."

"Of course you didn't, Lilly. And we didn't tell you kids because we knew you didn't need that burden. I'm only telling you now because I know what it's like to want a baby and not be able to have one. I feel for those couples, Lilly," he proclaimed, emotion thick in his voice. "Give that baby a chance."

Now she felt ashamed and she didn't even know why. Her mother's miscarriages weren't her fault. Yet, all the couples' needs weren't her problem either. "I'll think about adoption again."

"Thank you." His voice gentling, her dad squeezed her shoulder. "Before you know it, you'll be going off to college and all this will just be a memory."

That didn't give her any comfort. She didn't want to forget about the baby. And even though she and Alec were no more, she knew she'd never forget him either.

The kitchen felt stifling. Standing up, she took both their cereal bowls to the sink and rinsed them out. Looking at the clock, she mentally groaned. It was only nine thirty. She had a whole day in front of her with nothing to do. It was enough to slowly make her go crazy. "Dad, I'm going to go out for a little while, go take a walk."

"It's thirty degrees out. There's still snow on the ground. You'll need to dress warm."

Here she was, having a baby, making decisions that were going to determine the rest of her life — and her father was worried she didn't have enough sense to wear a coat. "It's sunny, though. Listen, I really need to get out of here. I turned in my algebra homework and don't have any assignments due for three days."

"If you wait until this evening when I get home from work, I could go with you."

"I need some time alone. You know I'm not used to being home all day, every day."

Looking her over, he seemed to sense that she was at her wit's end. "All right. But

134

choose a family? Please?"

"I'll try, Dad."

She really did need to get away from the house. She especially needed to get away from that adoption book! No matter where she was, it seemed to appear in whatever room she was in.

She needed to escape the questions and the prodding and everyone who acted like she was the dumbest person in the room. After throwing on her mom's roomy black wool coat and blue scarf and mittens, she walked down her driveway. From the moment the cool, crisp air fanned her face, she felt more relaxed and almost like herself.

Almost free. Chasing that feeling, she quickened her pace. In no time she was next to the hedge that divided their property from the Grabers'. She followed that to a well-worn path toward the river.

The winter grass crunched beneath her thick winter boots, sounding vaguely like broken glass as she walked along. As she quickened her pace, amazingly, her heart rate seemed to slow. Farther down, she spied a doe.

Lilly paused, eyeing the animal's beauty. Her eyes were black, and her fur was heavy and slightly shaggy, showing she'd grown a thick winter coat. Bit by bit, the deer raised her head and stared back at her but didn't budge.

Lilly stood as still as she was able, transfixed.

"Ach, but she's a fair sight, ain't she?"

With a start, Lilly spun around just as the deer darted off with a flick of her tail. "Josh."

"That's me." His lips curved up for a moment. "So, what are you doing out here?"

"Nothing. I was just out for a walk. What about you?"

He pointed to the west. "I was over at a neighbor's. Mrs. Slabaugh is a widow and every so often Caleb and I go over and chop wood for her. That's what I was doing this morning."

"And now you're on your way home."

"I am. It's quicker to return this way than to take a buggy."

"It's nice that you chop the wood for that lady."

He shrugged. "She needs the help, plus her daughter is the schoolteacher. We figure it's the least we can do since she has to put up with Anson all day," he added with a teasing smile. "Since I'm walking, too, would you care for some company?"

Unlike her father's offer, his interested her. *Why was that?* Curiously, she eyed him. He was so different from Alec. Different from Charlie, too. Than any boy she'd ever met before. More polite. Less full of rowdiness and pride. But maybe she didn't know him well at all. Maybe on the inside, he was the same as any of them. Of course, it didn't really matter.

And, perhaps, she was different than she used to be. "Sure."

"I'll walk you to the river. Have you been yet?"

"No. But I'm game if you are."

"Game?"

"You know, willing?"

"Oh. Yes, I am willing. I'm game." He looked at her shoes a bit doubtfully. "Will you be able to walk on the trails in those boots? They don't look like they'd stand up to a harsh wind."

Lilly couldn't help but be amused. What other boys asked about shoes? Holding up one of her feet she said, "Definitely. They're Sorels."

The look he gave her was priceless, and no less than she deserved. Obviously her sales pitch on the expensive shoes was wasted on him. "Never mind. I'll be fine. These kicks are sturdier than they look."

"Kicks?" That surprised a chuckle from him. "Ach. Maybe so. And, maybe you are sturdier than you look, as well."

"Maybe I am. Boy, that would make me so happy."

Joshua smiled then started off with little fanfare. Lilly jogged a bit to keep up with him, then easily found she could match her stride to his. With each step, the Grabers' house faded into the distance and brought her closer to another thicket of woods.

He wasn't one to talk much, which was fine with her. Lilly let her mind drift. For once, instead of focusing only on herself and her problems, she found herself noticing the beautiful surroundings. Just feeling peaceful for a change.

They continued. Soon, they reached a small valley. The natural lay of the land served to shield them from a bit of the wind, enabling the sun to shine down upon them and take the edge off of the chill. Their quick pace helped tremendously, too. A fine sheen of sweat formed on her brow.

As they walked along, Joshua pointed out a beaver eagerly chewing what was left of a log. "He's a hungry fella, that beaver is. Don'tcha think?"

Lilly slowed as she watched the animal chewing furiously on a tree trunk that had to be as big as her calf. Its dark brown coat looked almost like shiny tar, it was so glossy in the sunlight. "I've never seen a beaver before. I mean, not in the wild like this." She paused to think. "Maybe one was in a nature museum."

"Beavers, now they're a rascally bunch. Usually we think of them as a nuisance. But I've often enjoyed their antics. Always busy, you know."

"Busy is how I would describe you," Lilly commented. "From what I can tell, everyone in your family works hard."

"We've seven children. I'm the oldest. Next comes Judith, then Caleb. Anson, Carrie, Maggie, and finally Toby. He's three. In addition, we've got two pigs, chickens, a milk cow, and two horses. In the spring, my mamm plants a garden big enough to provide for us most all the year. With all of that, we can't help but be busy. Mamm wouldn't have it any other way."

The amount of work made her feel lazy. Here it was just a little after ten and Joshua had already chopped firewood. "And you've got your store."

"*Jah.* We've many blessings, it's true."

Lilly noticed he didn't seem too happy about it. "Why do I get the feeling you aren't happy about the store?"

For a moment, Lilly didn't think he was going to answer. Then, just as if he'd been hard-pressed to speak, he grudgingly said,

"Lilly, lately I've had something weighing on my mind, if you want to know the truth."

It was almost a relief to think about somebody else's problems. "Do you want to talk about it?"

"I should talk about it, yes."

Oh, he cracked her up. Everything was so literal. He never took anything between them for granted. "I mean, would you like to talk about it to *me?*"

"To you?"

"Sure, why not? I'm the perfect person to share things with. You hardly know me so you won't worry about me giving you my opinions. I'll just listen. Is it a relationship problem? I'm great at romance problems." In spite of her bold words, she winced. Actually, she hadn't been all that great at romance. If she had been, things would have probably worked out far differently with Alec.

"I'm not sure."

Lilly wasn't sure what he was replying to. Was he not sure he wanted to talk? Or was he not sure that it was a relationship problem?

The landscape grew rockier. When she stumbled, Joshua reached out and took hold of her elbow, steadying her with his warm grasp. That impersonal clutch made her do

140

a double-take. There was a connection between them. Something intense and personal. Like they were meant to be together. To be friends.

"Or, we don't have to talk," she said a good five minutes later — even though the silence was starting to get to her. "Just walking is fine."

"I'm worried about my future," he blurted. "I'm worried about my plans. And everyone else's plans for me, too."

Lilly was glad her face was averted. If he saw her surprise, he might be embarrassed. "What about it?"

"Lilly, do ya ever wonder if the plan everyone has for ya is truly God's plan?"

To be honest, she'd never had much thought about what God had in mind for her. All she'd been focused on was what she wanted, and what her parents wanted, and tried her best for the two needs to be the same.

Of course now, worrying about her future seemed to be a full-time occupation. Slowly she admitted, "I've wondered what kind of job I'm going to have. What kind of job I'd enjoy."

"And a partner?"

"A partner? You mean, like, a boyfriend or husband?" When he nodded, she continued.

"Of course I've thought about who I want to marry." Now that she let her guard down, disappointment coursed through her. Once, she'd had so many girlish dreams for herself and Alec. She'd fantasized about going to college with him. About getting engaged, then married, then one day planning their family. But those things were too hard to admit.

It was better to think about girlish dreams than bitter realities. Forcibly brightening her voice, she said, "When I was little, I used to spend hours thinking about my wedding. Planning every detail, from what kind of dress I'd wear to what my flowers would look like. Every girl does that, I suppose."

"I suspect you're right." Looking troubled, he said, "Do you think people ever change their minds about what they want? About who they want?"

Memories of her last argument with Alec rushed forward. There was only one reply. "Yes."

"But is that what God wants? I don't know."

"What's wrong, Josh?" His questions didn't seem merely curious. No, something specific was on his mind.

He didn't answer at first as they followed

the trail, walking around a stack of broken logs, passing a thicket of trees barren of leaves. Lilly struggled to keep up with his pace — his legs were longer and he was far more used to the area than she was.

Finally, after stepping carefully over a frozen patch of water, they slowed as the ground sloped down and the ground underfoot became more littered with stones and pebbles.

"See, for years, I've only thought about Gretta," he said softly.

She'd heard the name before. "She's your girlfriend, right?"

"She's my sweetheart, yes." He shook his head. "No, that's not right. She's been my almost sweetheart. Everyone assumed we'd be courting in earnest by now and planning our wedding."

"But not now?"

"I don't know about now. A few days ago I told Gretta that I wanted some time to think about things. I told her that I wasn't sure about her. About us."

"Wow." Lilly could only imagine how that had gone over. "What did she say?"

Looking completely puzzled, he said, "She said that she understood. That she would like some time, too." He hung his head. "I think there was more than that, though. I think she was mighty sad."

"I bet she was. But she might have been telling the truth. Girls have doubts and change their minds, too. So, are you happy that she let you off so easily?"

"That's the problem, I fear. See, I thought hearing that she understood would be good news, indeed. But it wasn't. I felt like maybe I wanted her to be missing me. Now, I just learned that Roland took her home the other day. I see that he's just been waiting for me to get out of the way." He paused, gathering his thoughts. "Perhaps that is how it's supposed to be? Perhaps she never really liked me as much as I thought she did."

He was jealous! Somehow that made Lilly feel even more secure in sharing her opinions — jealousy was a universal flaw. It certainly wasn't as hard to relate to as living an Amish life. "Trust me, if Roland has been around for a while and Gretta ignored him until recently, she only likes you."

Hope flared in his eyes before worry returned. "I don't know if Gretta thinks like that."

"If she's a girl, she does." When he frowned, she did a little more prodding. "What about you? Is there another girl that you're thinking of?"

"For a few days, it was you, Lilly," he

blurted.

In a flash, her mouth went dry. "Me?"

"Oh, *jah.* I looked at you and . . . wondered."

She was so completely embarrassed for the both of them, she wanted to run away. Yes, there was definitely something between them, a true connection, but she wasn't ready to try and figure out what exactly that was. She wasn't ready to fall in love again. She wasn't even ready to fall in "like" . . . "Josh," she began slowly . . . "I don't want to hurt your feelings, but I don't —"

"Oh, I don't fancy you." He laughed. "I realized that as soon as I prayed about it."

In spite of the prim little lecture she'd been about to give him, she felt a little disappointed. "Oh."

"After all, we wouldn't suit. You're English."

"I know. You're Amish, by the way."

Smiling softly, he said, "We could never make a match. I don't fancy being an *Englischer* . . . and somehow I don't see you eager to be Amish neither."

"Then what were you thinking about me? If, you know, you weren't thinking that you wanted to, you know . . ."

"Go courting?"

"Yes. Go courting."

"It's like this. Lilly, if seeing you turns my head, if seeing you makes me think of different things, if being with you makes me doubt my future with Gretta . . . then something's gotta be wrong, don'tcha think?"

"I don't know." Thinking of Alec — and how sweet he was until she asked for more than he could give — she murmured, "Sometimes people change. Sometimes the things we want take us by surprise and then we don't know how to deal with it."

"You do understand."

"I do. Unfortunately."

They'd finally stopped next to the wide creek. All her worries about the future faded as she gazed at its simple beauty. It was so peaceful. Deer tracks decorated the snowy banks, but that was the only sign that other creatures had visited it as well. Large sections of the creek bed were frozen solid. A spattering of snow decorated the top like coconut on a cake.

But in other areas, only a thin layer of ice separated the water from the outside air. The ice was so thin and transparent, she saw a running current flowing smooth over the rocks.

It made her think of their lives. Of how some parts were so stable and fixed, nothing could penetrate them. But other areas were far thinner. They might look solid, but the fragile layers were easily broken. In transition. And in those parts, why anything was possible. Ice could return . . . or it could all melt away.

Next to her, Josh also looked intrigued by the water. Finally, he spoke. "Lilly, I feel it's as if God gave me a little push into this terribly cold water, shaking me up. Wakening up my feelings."

"Giving you an awakening."

He nodded. "*Jah.* And now that I'm so awake, I hardly know what to do. Everything before seems too quiet."

Thinking of the baby, Lilly realized that she, too, felt the same way. "I've had an awakening, too," she said slowly. For a moment, she was tempted to tell him about the pregnancy, about Alec's stunned expression when she'd told him. About how embarrassed and ashamed she'd been to tell her parents. About how alone she'd felt when she realized that the new life growing inside her was also ending their relationship.

About everyone's determination that she should have this baby and move on and forget that she'd ever been pregnant. But she didn't dare voice the words. It was too difficult.

And too much of a secret. Besides, what would she do if Josh was so shocked by her circumstances that he abandoned her, too? She didn't think she could bear it. For once she felt like she had someone to talk to.

"What was your awakening?"

She told what she could. "Oh, about what you'd expect. I've been trying to figure out the rest of my life. And, moving here has been really hard, too. It's really different from Cleveland. Sugarcreek is so small."

"It has everything you'd ever need, though."

"I suppose it does . . . for some people."

"But not for you?"

"No. Well, at least I don't think so." Reaching out, she squeezed his hand. "But it's not all bad. We met."

"Yes. Perhaps one day we could be friends."

"I'd like that, Josh. I could use a friend." She felt her muscles relax as she looked at their clasped hands. For just a moment longer, she took time to enjoy how secure her mittened hand felt in his heavy, work-hardened one.

After another reassuring squeeze, Josh dropped his hand. "Let's go back, yes?"

"Yes."

As they walked along, she couldn't resist teasing him. "So, you really never thought about dating me? After you prayed on it, I mean?"

"Dating?"

"Come on, you know. Courting." She leaned closer, nudged him with her shoulder. "Hugging. Kissing. You never thought about kissing me?"

To her amusement he glanced at her lips, and was evidently weighing the pros and cons of his interest in her . . . right there to her face. "I'm sorry but no. I've had no interest in kissing you at all." His words and tone were solemn.

But his eyes were merry.

"Liar. I bet you've thought about kissing me. I've thought about kissing you."

"And?"

"I don't think we'd enjoy it at all, Joshua Graber. I, uh, hope you don't mind."

"Not at all. It's a fair relief I won't be having to fend you off, and that's a fact."

As they continued the long trek back to their homes, Lilly found herself laughing more than she had in six months. Found herself chatting and sharing things with Josh . . . things she never imagined ever telling another person.

"I best go to work now."

"Yes. I, um, have things to do also."

After all the stress and all the arguing . . . Joshua Graber was making her life bearable.

And for that, she knew she'd always be grateful.

She felt warm and secure . . . until she saw her mother staring through one of the front windows of the house. And she was glaring at her in disbelief.

CHAPTER 10

"Have a care," Caleb warned under his breath just as Joshua closed the kitchen door behind him later that evening. "Mamm and Daed aren't none too happy."

He barely had a moment to stare at his brother somewhat dumbly before his father marched up to him, eyes full of fire.

"Joshua, you were seen walking with that *Englischer* this morning. Seen walking together hand in hand near the river."

He couldn't help but be puzzled by his father's tone. Trying to unscramble the accusations, he pulled off his black felt hat and rubbed his head. "*Englischer?* Oh, you mean Lilly?"

"Son, don't sound so confused. You know whom I speak of. Of course I am speaking about Lilly Allen."

Behind their father, Caleb shook his head in a well-practiced sign of warning.

Joshua still didn't understand what he was

in trouble about. "What about her?"

His father's usual calm demeanor went walking as his anger roared to life. "What about her? Don't play such games with me, Joshua. You sit down here and talk to me."

Joshua winced. Yes, he most certainly should've been more circumspect. Hastily, he sat. And waited. After a moment, Caleb kicked his boot. "Say something, *bruder.*"

His father narrowed his eyes and crossed his arms over his chest. For sure, his patience had neared its end.

So Josh started talking. "I meant to say yes, I was walking with Lilly this morning before I went to work."

"We told you at supper that we didn't want you spending any more time with her. She is not for you, Joshua."

"I know that. We're just friends, that's all."

His father's steel gray eyes flashed. "You have friends. Plenty of Amish friends. You don't need her."

He knew different. When he thought about how well Lilly had listened when he'd admitted his feelings for Gretta . . . when he thought of how helpful she'd tried to be . . . Joshua knew that he needed her something awful. She was a friend he wanted to have for many years into the future. "I think otherwise."

"Should we forbid you to see her, then?"

"No. Course not," he said slowly, weighing each word with care.

Joshua wished he could see more of his brother than just his profile. Then he'd be able to get a bit more information. The Graber family knew many among the English. They counted more than a handful as friends. Both of his parents spoke often of their old neighbors, the Wilsons. What had set their father off?

"It's time you became baptized, son. It's more than past. It's time you put away your running-around years, and stopped your questions and worries. It's time you grew up and became part of the community and put childish notions aside. You need to accept your life, and accept your responsibility to it."

It took everything Joshua had inside him not to counter each of his father's statements just to clarify things. He most certainly had not been "running around" in years.

Plus, all he did was work at home and at the store. If that was not accepting responsibility, he didn't know what was!

Oh, but he wanted to speak up for himself, to counter his father's lists of his failings. However, Joshua didn't need his brother's frantic hand signals to let him know that it was time to be quiet.

And, well, he'd been planning to tell his parents he was ready to be baptized soon anyway. "I agree, Father," he replied almost meekly, when his father finally drew a breath. "I'll get baptized soon."

One peppered black eyebrow rose. "You will?"

"I will. I will talk to the bishop and the church leaders on Sunday. I'm finally ready."

"Gut." Looking like a balloon that had just lost all its air, his father nodded. With a small weary sigh, he stood up, turned on his heel, then walked down the stairs to the basement.

When they were alone, Josh sighed and leaned back in his chair. "Thanks for the warning, but I think I could have used it a little bit earlier. Daed was surely in a fine temper."

"That's because Mamm was fit to be tied. She's been so worried that Lilly Allen has turned your head. Someone saw the two of you together talking by the river and thought of the worst."

Joshua rolled his eyes. "And the worst was that she and I might like each other?"

"To Mamm, that would be terribly bad.

You know that."

"I'm sorry she was worried, but things will be fine."

"Are you sure?"

"All we've become is friends. Mamm and Daed shouldn't have any worries about Lilly and I being more than that. Ever."

"Are you back to Gretta, then?"

Caleb never did watch his tongue! But though Joshua had an urge to tell him to mind his own business, after talking things through with Lilly, Joshua was starting to realize that he'd been trying to do too much on his own instead of praying and waiting for God to lead him to the right path. "Gretta suits me," he added. "She and I will most likely be happy together."

"But you're not positive?"

"No."

After Caleb thought on that for a bit, he said, "You know, it is *gut* that you are joining the church now. Finally. It's time. I mean, if that's what you want."

Something in his brother's tone made Joshua look at Caleb a little more closely. "Why wouldn't it be?"

This time it was Caleb who looked like he would like to be dodging questions. "No reason. It's just that some people don't ever join, you know."

"Some don't, but I can't think of a member of our family who hasn't been baptized."

"One day I bet someone will change his mind and won't."

"I doubt it." For his part, Joshua couldn't even imagine such a thing. Being Amish was who they were. He might have questions about who to marry or what to do, but never about that. "I hope I'm not around to see Daed's face if that happens," he joked. "Can you imagine how angry he'd be?"

But instead of grinning, Caleb only stared at him with solemn eyes. "Yes, I can. I can imagine his anger perfectly."

What did one say about a sweetheart who no longer thought you were good enough? That's what Gretta wanted to know. She sure was needing that answer something awful, now that her love life was the focus of most every conversation.

The gossips were full of themselves in the shops and in the restaurant, too. Even Miriam had had quite a bit to say about Gretta taking a ride in Roland's buggy.

Just this morning Gretta had struggled to redirect most every conversation that Miriam had started. It seemed that all conversational roads began and ended with Joshua Graber.

156

Or Roland Schrock.

Or both.

She was right tired of it all.

The frosty atmosphere permeating everything at home was not a help either. Though her father had reassured her that they both only wanted her happy, Gretta wasn't so sure.

More than ever, she wished her mother would step aside and not interfere so much. Lately she'd had something to say about everything and it didn't matter if Gretta wanted to hear about her opinions or not.

This day was no different.

From the moment Gretta had stepped inside that afternoon, she was peppered with questions about her intentions for the future. It was as if her mother was feeling nervous about Gretta not having a wedding one day! That she would become a *maidal,* an old maid.

Supper had been no easier. Once again her parents hardly spoke to each other. As each bite was consumed, the tension seemed to increase tenfold. And while heavy silence wasn't unusual, feeling as if she was the reason was new.

Earlier, Gretta had heard snippets of their arguing through their closed bedroom door. Her father had berated Mamm for meddling in Gretta's life too much. In contrast, her mother had been mighty irritated by her father's lack of interest in Gretta's married life.

By suppertime, stony silence had reigned. By the time their four plates were clean, the air was thick and stifling and she and Margaret had been eager to go wash everyone's dishes.

Later, when her father went out to the barn and her mother sought comfort in her quilting, Gretta took refuge in the peaceful comfort of her room. As she gazed at her quilt, pieced together in pretty shades of pink and violet and yellow, she felt her body finally relax.

As far as she was concerned, she would be happy to stay in her room for the night. Yes, indeed, she could do any number of things in the quiet privacy of her room. During her lunch, she'd gone to the bookstore and bought a new book. She also had a pair of socks she was knitting for the homeless shelter in the community.

And then, of course, there were the sayings she was embroidering on linen napkins for the farmers' market. If she worked hard, she could certainly complete another one that evening. Those always brought in a good price.

Yes, there was much to do besides moon over Roland and Joshua. Or worry that one of them would bring her to a life like her parents', where there was little laughter and not much else.

Not ten minutes later, a knock at their front door brought all thoughts of sitting quietly to a stop. Her mother's burst of surprise to see their visitors, along with Margaret calling for Gretta to join them, brought her to her feet. Hopping up quickly, Gretta ventured out into the hall. Who could be paying them a call?

She came to an abrupt stop when she saw who it was. Joshua's family?

There was Elsa and Judith Graber and little Maggie Graber, too. When they spied her, Mrs. Graber's full cheeks lifted into a smile. "There you are, Gretta. I hope you don't mind, but we decided to come for a visit."

"She — I mean we — don't mind at all," her mother said before Gretta even had time to open her mouth. "I'll go make a fresh pot of coffee and slice up some banana bread. Gretta take our guests into the sitting room."

Feeling awkward, Gretta smiled Judith's way as she led them into the room. Luckily her mother had just lit a fire so it was cozy

159

and warm.

"How have you all been?" she asked.

Judith smiled. "We've been missing you. It's been mighty strange not seeing you every now and then."

Gretta felt her cheeks heat. Not only had she missed Joshua, she'd missed his wonderful, noisy family, too. "I feel the same way," she replied, meaning every word. Unable to help herself, she murmured, "How is Joshua?"

Mrs. Graber frowned. "He says he is okay, but I don't know if that is true. I'm concerned with some of his decisions of late, if you want to know the truth."

Gretta didn't know how to reply. Though she, too, had felt a bit worried about their future, she'd never dared to voice her thoughts. Not like he had.

Crawling off of the couch, little Maggie ran over to Gretta and held out her arms. "Hi, Gretta!"

Gretta gave the four-year-old a hug as she settled Maggie on her lap. "Hi. You look like you've gotten bigger."

"Mamm says that, too."

They chuckled as her mother came back in with a tray full of filled coffee cups and sliced bread. After serving them all, she took a seat next to Gretta. "So what are we going to do about our *kinner?* I keep telling Gretta to do more to try to get Joshua's attention."

Mrs. Graber blinked before replying. "I don't think that is what he needs," she said slowly with a sweet look Gretta's way. "After all, Gretta is just fine how she is. It's Joshua who's been in a difficult place, I think."

"He's found a friend in Lilly Allen, that's what's happened," Judith said bluntly.

"You need to keep them apart," Gretta's mother warned. "She'll turn his head."

Hearing the blame heaped on Joshua's shoulders shamed her. "Joshua has not been the only one to want to look around some," Gretta felt compelled to add. "After all, it is his right. Nothing has been decided."

Mrs. Graber nodded. "Perhaps you're right, dear. We've heard about Roland. Do you find that you fancy him?"

With her mother, Judith, and Mrs. Graber all looking at her, Gretta felt more embarrassed than ever. Even little Maggie was looking at her curiously. "I don't know. I want a husband who suits me. Roland might . . . or he might not. Josh and me looking around is not a bad thing. We've known each other a long time. It might be a mistake to step forward into marriage without considering life with other people. Marriage is forever, you know."

Her gaze softening, Mrs. Graber nodded. "I wanted to let you know that Joshua has agreed to get baptized soon, praise the good Lord. I think that is a good sign, yes? Perhaps things will get straightened out soon."

"Maybe they will."

"If you stop thinking about Roland Schrock," her mother stated.

Thankfully, Mrs. Graber didn't acknowledge her mother's rude behavior. "Gretta, we just wanted you to know that we still care for you. We still want you to come by to visit us. Even if things never work out between you and Joshua."

"Please do, Gretta. I've missed you," Judith chimed in with a smile.

"I've missed you, too. I'm so glad you all came by today."

"Me too?" Maggie asked.

Reaching out to tickle one of Maggie's ribs, Gretta grinned. "Especially you."

Whether on purpose or happenstance, the two older women left the room to look at quilts, giving Judith and Gretta some time to visit more privately.

As soon as the other women were out of earshot, Judith leaned forward. "So, truly . . . are you serious about Roland?"

"I'm not sure."

"He's always seemed a bit dull to me."

"He's caring and tries hard."

Judith wrinkled her nose. "I suppose."

It was on the tip of Gretta's tongue to re-assure Judith that her heart was only Joshua's. But she was afraid to hope . . . and afraid to pass up her chance for a marriage.

She couldn't deny that she and Joshua had done nothing but argue for the last week or two of their relationship. She didn't want a future like her parents, full of anger and recriminations and frosty mealtimes. Instead, she longed for a peaceful home. With Roland, Gretta thought there was a good chance she could have that.

But no matter what happened, she didn't intend to sit and wait and simply hope that things would get better. She wanted to begin her life. To leave her parents' house and all the painful memories that festered there. To start anew.

And if that meant accepting a man who might be a little quiet and boring, then, well, so be it.

"I think Joshua might be for me, but I'm just not sure. Roland Schrock has many qualities, too," she confided. It was hard to compare someone she'd been close to for years with someone she'd only spent a few moments with.

"Yes, but Joshua and you are meant to be together. I know it."

Gretta wanted to believe that, but she wasn't so sure. "My heart does care deeply for Joshua, but I'm not sure what my mind says about our life together."

"I have a feeling your life with him will be how our house is now, Gretta," Judith said softly, letting Gretta know that she knew far more about Gretta's circumstances than she'd ever let on. "You'll have laughter and love. You might have disagreements, but you'll have other things too. Passion and warmth and happiness."

Stunned at Judith's words, Gretta stared at her friend. Were those things important? Would she one day tire of steadiness and peace and yearn for laughter and arguments and . . . passion?

When Maggie hopped off the couch and ran toward the kitchen, Judith stood as well, to make sure the little girl didn't run into trouble. "Don't forget that quiet doesn't always equal happiness, Gretta," she said in parting. "Sometimes a quiet home is simply a place where no one has anything to say. And that would be a *verra* sad place to be, I would think."

"I'll remember," Gretta murmured.

CHAPTER 11

As far as Lilly's family was concerned, she was turning a bad situation into a lifelong mistake. Ever since she'd tearfully told her parents she was pregnant, they'd wanted to take charge of her, to make everything better.

Since she was obviously not capable of doing anything right.

She didn't agree.

As she stared at the cell phone in her hand, Lilly knew she was doing the right thing for herself, and for her baby. It was time to grow up and respect herself and her own beliefs.

After punching the seven digits in her phone, she pressed Send and waited. Then Ms. Vonn picked up much too soon. "Hi, Lilly," she said as soon as the introductions were over with. "How can I help you?"

"I just wanted to let you know that I won't be needing your services anymore."

In the background, Lilly heard Ms. Vonn's chair squeak as she got more comfortable. "Why won't you?"

"Because . . . because I'm going to keep the baby. I've made my decision," she said quickly, before she lost her nerve.

"Did you patch things up with . . ." Her voice drifted off as she shuffled papers. "Alec?"

"No. He's not involved in this decision."

"What about your parents?"

"This is my decision," Lilly said firmly, not daring to share the fact that she hadn't told them about her change of heart. "I've made up my mind. It's final."

"I see." After a pause, Ms. Vonn said, "Well, thank you for calling, Lilly. I'll go ahead and inform those couples that you won't be choosing any of them."

Ms. Vonn sounded so sad for the other people, Lilly almost gave in. Almost.

But then she remembered the little flutter she'd felt inside of her belly just that morning. And she thought of how sick she'd felt even thinking about never holding her baby.

Never being its mom.

She hardened her voice. "Well, I guess that's all I wanted to say."

"Don't forget that you can always change your mind . . . it's a big decision, no one will be upset if you do."

But she'd be upset with herself. She knew it as well as she knew she still liked Disney movies and hated the freckles on her nose. "I won't," Lilly said before hanging up. This was one thing she wasn't going to change her mind about.

After hanging up and taking a deep breath, she pushed the number seven on her phone and waited for Alec Wagoner's familiar ring tone to sound.

"Lilly?" he said as soon as he picked up.

"Yep."

"Hey. What's going on?"

In the privacy of her room, she rolled her eyes. He sounded so casual, like they'd just seen each other that morning. "Oh, the usual. I'm still living in Sugarcreek. Still finishing up high school online."

"And . . . are you still, you know?"

He sounded so hopeful that she wasn't that it was almost funny. "Pregnant? Yeah."

"Oh. Well, is everything okay?"

"Yeah. Listen I just wanted to tell you that I'm going to keep the baby, but I don't need you to be around. Okay?"

"You don't want to put it up for adoption anymore?" Panic laced his words.

"No. I just can't, Alec."

"I'm going to college —"

"I want you to go," she said in a rush, eager to say her peace and get off the phone. "Believe me, I know we're done. I just wanted to, you know, tell you. I'll have my dad's lawyer write something up so you won't have to do anything, okay?"

"Oh. Okay. Sure."

Well, there was nothing left to say. "See you, Alec. Bye."

For a moment, he paused. Lilly closed her eyes, waiting to hear something special from him. Something about how he really had cared about her. Or how everything that they'd been hadn't been a total mistake.

Her breath caught. Waiting.

"Well . . . bye, Lilly," he finally said.

She hung up, too. Then flopped down on her bed.

Her life with Alec was over.

To her surprise, the realization brought a rush of tears to her eyes. For so long, he had been just one of her brother's friends who had been especially cute. Then, two years ago, she'd developed the biggest crush on him. Though Charlie had teased her, Alec had merely looked flattered.

And then he'd asked her to the winter dance. From then on, they'd been together all the time. Only after they'd had sex did things start getting confusing. She'd thought they were falling in love.

Alec, she later found out, had been ready to move on. Her pregnancy had propelled him forward even faster.

And now . . . he was part of her past. He wanted it that way.

Even though she was having his baby.

Josh figured the Lord had been with him and Lilly the other day when they'd met and gone walking together. He'd needed someone to talk to. And talking to her had made him feel better in a way that nothing else had.

Which was a fair bit disturbing. He was close to his family members and knew he could count and depend on them for most anything. Never had he imagined feeling such ease with a woman. Never had he imagined he could be friends with a woman, and especially a woman so different from himself.

But Lilly Allen was his friend. Her ears had seemed to understand his problems and worries about Gretta. Perhaps because she didn't know everyone very well, she'd been more free to offer insight than most people he'd known for his whole life. He was glad of her help, but truly confused about why

169

the Lord had placed her to be his confidante.

The few days that had passed since their walk had been busy ones. He'd worked at the store two afternoons and then spent most of the past evening helping to chop more firewood.

And butchering two hens for some *Englischers* who visited the store often. His family didn't usually provide fresh poultry for their customers, but his parents liked the Olsons very much and had offered the hens when Mrs. Olson had announced she was throwing a dinner party for her newly engaged son.

Joshua had a sneaky suspicion that his daed had sent him to do the butchering as a bit of punishment because of his relationship with Lilly.

And it might have been a punishment, indeed. Everyone in the family knew he got queasy killing chickens.

Now a full week had passed since his walk to the river and he was working at the store's cash register. Caleb was standing nearby, being his usual difficult self.

"When are you going to ask Charlie for another ride in his truck?" he asked for what was surely the third time that day.

"I don't know."

"I hope it's soon. You said yourself that you and Lilly are *gut* friends. Just go ask him."

"But I have no need for a ride."

"Well, I do. I need to go to town. I met some English teens the other day. They like to go to McDonalds."

Joshua snorted. "You make everything the *Englischers* do sound special. It isn't, you know."

"You only say that because you get to do so much."

"I've been killing chickens and working at the store," Joshua reminded him with more than a touch of sarcasm. "I wouldn't call it so much."

"Don't forget Lilly. You two went walking last week."

"That was on accident. Our paths just happened to cross. And, you know what happened afterward. Mamm and Daed are still grumpy with me."

"Maybe they'll cross again soon?"

Oh, but Caleb's voice was softly insinuating. "I don't feel romantic toward her, I told you that."

"But feelings could change. Do you think you'll like her one day? One day like her more than Gretta?"

"No." Joshua felt his skin flush as he realized just how quickly he'd come up with that response. He still did have feelings for Gretta. Strong feelings. Feelings that seemed to be growing as they'd kept their distance.

What had been wrong with him lately?

"Me and Lilly are just friends," he said again. "We're too different to be anything more anyway."

"Different in ways besides her being English?"

"Yes. Though that's different enough."

By his side, Caleb looked for a moment like he was going to dispute that. But he held his tongue.

Joshua was very glad about that. He was tired of everyone in his family weighing in on his love life. What he felt for Gretta was a private thing. As far as he was concerned, no one else needed to know about it.

He was just about to say that out loud when the front door opened and the bells at the handle rang through the store.

Caleb looked like he'd just struck gold. "Well, look who's here."

Joshua frowned as Gretta entered the store with her friend Miriam. Gretta's cheeks bloomed as she nodded in his direction before hooking her girlfriend's arm and scuttling down toward the dry goods.

As they faded from his view, Joshua felt

172

somewhat taken aback. In the past, she'd approached him the moment she'd walked in. Always before, she'd stood anxiously near him, waiting for his attention, eager for his words.

There'd been many a time he hadn't been too kind about her attention. He'd be busy and she'd want to talk. Or he'd be taking a breather and she'd act like he needed more to do. But always he'd counted on her attention — even if he hadn't been quite so eager to return the favor.

Now he was ashamed to realize that he'd begun to take her for granted. Now he felt bereft because he was only receiving the very slightest of nods.

"You're in trouble now, brother," Caleb whispered. "Gretta sure doesn't want much to do with you today."

"Perhaps she's simply in a hurry."

As they saw Gretta dart along a back aisle, steadfastly not looking their way, Caleb dared to grin. "*Bruder,* no one's ever in that big of a hurry."

Before he could weigh the pros and cons of it, Joshua found himself walking out from behind the counter going toward the women. "Stay here," he ordered Caleb, just in case he got an idea to get in the way.

"I'll be happy to," Caleb answered as

173

another pair of customers entered the store.

Feeling better now that Caleb was occupied, Joshua combed the aisles for Gretta, finally finding her with all the sugar and spices. "Gretta, are you finding everything all right?"

She barely looked up. "I am."

That was all she was going to say? Wordlessly, he looked to Miriam. She stared right back at him with wide eyes. Too innocently, he thought.

Feeling a bit silly, he leaned against one of the wide wooden posts. She'd have to weave a wide path around him if she was determined to leave.

"So, how are things at the Sugarcreek Inn?"

"They are fine."

"I've been meaning to stop by, I just haven't had the chance . . ."

Finally looking directly at him, Gretta almost smiled. "Don't worry, Joshua. You don't need to visit me. I — I don't hardly look for you anymore."

"Oh. I see." Her words were no more than what he deserved, but still, they felt painful and terribly sharp. Although . . . there had been a stammer in her voice. Maybe she wasn't as unaffected by him as she acted?

Blue eyes searching, she murmured, "Do

174

you, Joshua?" Before he could form a phrase to reply, she cleared her throat. "Anyway, Miriam and I only stopped in the store to get some rice for dinner. My mother asked me to stop on my way home to get it."

"I'll get the rice for you. You want a one-pound bag?"

"No, we'll be needing five pounds. A group of us are going to make rice pudding this weekend."

Not long ago, she used to invite him over for rice pudding. But now, once again, no invitation was issued. "Well, then I'll go get you your five pounds of rice."

"Danke." Turning to Miriam, she said, "Did you want anything else?"

"No."

"I'll be needin' nothing else from you."

"I see." Just as she was turning away from him, he blurted, "Gretta, are you walking home today?" He already knew Miriam lived only two blocks away.

"I am."

"I bet I could drive you home in the buggy so you won't have to carry the rice."

She almost smiled. Almost. "It's only five pounds, Joshua. I'm no fancy English girl, *jah?* I think I'll be fine carrying my load."

"Oh. Then I guess I'll be seeing you at church, then."

"Yes, you will." After paying Caleb, she put the rice in a sturdy canvas bag she'd brought with her and fastened her cape at her neck a bit more securely.

When their eyes met one more time, she nodded. "*Gut* afternoon, Joshua. Good afternoon, and good day."

Speechless, he nodded right back, struggling to keep his expression still and quiet. But inside, his emotions were in turmoil. Oh, but he was so confused about his feelings. Now that Gretta was acting so cool, his insides were aching for one of her smiles.

He hoped she'd treat him to one on Sunday.

CHAPTER 12

The line was going slow because of Jacob's grandfather. Old Mr. Kempfs never failed to spark a conversation wherever he went, and the line for lunch after services must have seemed as good a time as any to catch up on the latest news.

As everyone waited in a long line around the perimeter of the barn, the weather was commented on as well as a new remedy someone had heard about for toothaches.

Gretta tried to look as if the minor interruption didn't bother her at all, but in truth, she was more than a bit chilly, standing as near as she was to the barn's opening. The metal building, so much easier for the farmers to install nowadays, was in most ways a mighty good spot for church services and a luncheon. But there was no insulation against the cold.

In addition, her head was aching something fierce. All she wanted to do was have her bowl of soup and sandwich and go sit down.

Finally Jacob's grandfather patted a youngster on the head, said goodbye, and went off to sit with the other men at the far back table and the line started moving again.

Beside her, Miriam was chatting to her sister, Ruth, about a dinner Ruth was hosting for her in-laws. Usually, Gretta would be eager to hear the details of the meal, and to offer some suggestions, too. Used to be, every so often she'd put herself to sleep at night imagining all the kinds of dinners that she'd cook for her own in-laws.

But now her future was all topsy-turvy, like someone had pulled a rug out from under her feet. She was finding it difficult to keep her bearings. All she wanted was to get her lunch and sit down.

The line inched closer. Ahead of her, she heard her mother exclaim over the potato salad of Jenna Seitz. Gretta frowned. Jenna always did know how to put just the right amount of sugar and vinegar in her salad. She, herself, had never mastered that. Hers was always too sweet or too tangy.

Most days her failed attempts didn't bother her. Now, though, it seemed to be yet one more source of aggravation.

Finally they approached the two long tables where everything was spread out. Gretta picked up a bowl and plate. Following the others, she passed over the peanut butter spread put out for the children. Instead, she ladled in a portion of vegetable soup and placed some trail bologna, freshly sliced bread, pickles, relish, and salad on her plate, then followed the others to the women's row of benches.

In the summer, many of the young people liked to sit together outside. More than once she and Miriam had brought along a quilt and sat with girlfriends under the trees, enjoying the day and the opportunities to visit and catch up with friends. The day would be made perfect when Joshua would join her — sometimes with his siblings Judith or Caleb, and sometimes with friends.

Of course, in the winter it wasn't near as easy to find a quiet place. And here in the Seitz barn with the metal walls, there could surely be no louder place around for miles. The noise from everyone's chatter felt deafening.

And all the talk — at least to Gretta's way of thinking — seemed to be centered around her and Joshua. Everyone seemed to know that they weren't a courting couple anymore.

Though she tried not to turn her head, she couldn't help but look Joshua's way when she walked by his table to her own. He was sitting next to his brother Caleb and a few other boys. His cheeks were rosy and he was laughing at someone's joke.

As she passed him, he conspicuously put his head down and averted his eyes. Gretta wondered if it was in retaliation for her frosty attitude when she'd visited his family's store.

All the elation she'd felt from turning down his offer of a buggy ride had faded when she'd walked home alone, carrying that big bag of rice.

At first she'd been so proud of herself for being aloof and strong in the store, but as each foot stepped in front of the other, she'd known she should have given Joshua a chance. She knew she should have graciously accepted his offer. They could have used the time to visit. And Gretta could have asked a few more questions about his relationship with the *Englischer,* to see if all the newest rumors about him going walking with Lilly Allen were true.

But she'd been unwilling to have her parents see that Joshua was driving her home once again. She'd known that her mother would ask a dozen questions and she would be forced to answer them. Then there would have been a good chance that a fight would erupt between her parents and they'd end the day in silence once again. Just like it had ended the evening before.

Yes, that had been the main reason, but not the only one. She'd also let her cursed pride take over.

Of course, giving into such sins had come with consequences. She'd been lonely walking by herself, and had quickly discovered that even five pounds of rice became a burden after a few blocks.

Now, walking by his table, Gretta, too, kept her head averted. There was no point trying to make things better at the moment. Especially not in front of their entire community.

"How can Joshua sit there, looking so happy?" Miriam said a little too loudly once they'd seated themselves and said a quick prayer of thanks. "Everyone knows he broke your heart."

"He didn't break it all by himself. He had some help from me," Gretta whispered. "We need to be quiet about it here, though. I've no desire for anyone to hear our private conversation." *Again,* she silently added, remembering how their "private" conversation had eventually found its way to Joshua's ears. Unfortunately, her girlfriend didn't have any desire to either lower her voice or stop talking. "I've heard Joshua is much sadder when he's not here, among friends." Looking superior, Miriam added, "I heard the news from Jenna, who heard it from Judith Graber herself."

"Well, it's *gut* to know our community's gossip mills are running well." Listlessly, Gretta took another bite of potato salad.

Miriam ignored the jab. "What are you going to do?"

"I don't know." Hoping to turn the tables, Gretta asked, "So, who has caught your eye lately? I didn't notice who you paired off with during the last Sunday's singing."

Completely ignoring the question, Miriam's voice rose. "But you should know who you fancy now, Gretta. This is an important thing, jah?"

It was too important for her to speak about it in the middle of their luncheon. "Let's not speak any more of this."

"But Gretta —"

"Please, Miriam. You don't know how badly my head is pounding. Besides, my mamm has already taken to darting a half dozen looks my way. She's going to pepper me good with questions for the whole buggy ride home."

"Ach, she will."

Little by little, the din in the room slowly subsided as a few of the older couples began to take their leave. Since Gretta had been one of the last to be served, she stayed put, slowly eating her lunch though she didn't taste a bit of it.

But then, as another hush flowed around her, and as Miriam giggled behind a napkin, Gretta looked up.

And only saw those lovely grayish green eyes of Joshua. He was standing before her, calm as you please. "Maybe I could take you home, Gretta?"

She was tempted. But she was afraid of those temptations. Before, she'd felt her future was secure with Joshua. Before, she'd never doubted her feelings for him . . . or his for her. But now things had changed. She no longer felt blind devotion toward him. Now she realized that things with Joshua might never be without conflict.

And that sometimes he could be terribly selfish.

And sometimes . . . so could she.

Now she needed some space and time as well. She needed to determine what would be best for herself. She couldn't do it sitting next to Joshua.

If she gave in to her desires, if she took a

turn with him in his buggy, chances were good that she'd soon be forgetting everything that was wrong between them. If she sat by his side, sharing a quilt and exchanging laughter, in no time at all she'd be eager for his smiles. Start eagerly waiting for him to stop by her home. To compliment her on her cooking. Anxious to plan her future again. *Their* future again.

She didn't dare accept his offer.

"Not today, Joshua."

"Oh. Well, all right." Rocking a bit on his heels, he murmured, "Gretta, how about we sit together for a bit right now? We have some things to talk about, I imagine."

Around them, time seemed to stop as everyone listened for her reply. Gretta knew what would happen if she did accept Joshua's offer. Someone would somehow find a way to eavesdrop on them. All people needed was snippets of their conversation to start gossiping. Living in their close community, everything that happened was fodder for speculation and interpretation.

And everything always had a way of getting back to her mother.

"Joshua, I don't think sitting with you would be a good idea."

"You sure?"

"I am. We needed a break, yes?" He

184

looked so confused, so helpless, so hand-some, she almost changed her mind. His eyes always did find a way to pierce through any resistance. To penetrate her heart. It reminded her of how much Joshua always was able to see and understand beyond words.

After a moment he nodded. "All right, then. Maybe another time."

"Maybe so. Or . . . maybe not."

When he looked at her in surprise before turning and walking away, Gretta almost blushed. Being so snippy was not her way. But at the moment, she didn't think she wanted to be any way else.

Certainly not a person to be played games with or pitied.

Definitely not to be pitied. She had some pride. She still remembered just how she'd felt when Joshua had said he wanted a break between them. She'd felt like her heart was breaking.

She just hoped he missed her sometimes, as much as she knew she missed him.

She'd just placed her napkin on her plate when Miriam coughed a warning. "What now?"

Miriam's eyes were gleeful. "Oh, Gretta, look who's walkin' your way!"

Following her friend's not-so-subtle finger

point, Gretta inwardly groaned. Oh, for heaven's sakes!

To her consternation, there was Roland Schrock, making a beeline right for her.

"Hi, there, Gretta."

"Hello, Roland. Good day."

"The weather is nice. It's not too cold. Perhaps you'd like to go for a buggy ride with me?"

She'd been cold all morning. She had a headache. She was confused and irritable.

But as she looked into his brown eyes, Gretta recalled his kindness the other day. In addition, she remembered just how she'd defended him to her mother. Surely she hadn't defended Roland simply to give her mother trouble?

Was she at all interested in Roland? She should at least try to be, Gretta supposed. He was the type of man she'd been praying to have in her life. He was so stable. He didn't ask much of her. Not like Joshua, who made her mad and anxious. Who could make her heart beat a little too fast with one slow, meaningful look.

Who could also crush her spirits with one unkind comment. Who also had been seen spending time with that English neighbor of his.

Sternly, she told herself that it was most

186

definitely time to think of the future instead of the past. "Why yes, Roland, I would like to take a ride with you. It sounds mighty nice."

Roland smiled and lifted his chin a bit more. "I would like that. You can tell your mother that I'll bring you home, too."

Well, where else would he be bringing her? She thought somewhat peevishly. Then she recalled she was trying to encourage him. And that she wanted to be a good Christian woman, too. "I will tell Mamm that. *Danke*."

Around her, the air was thick with anticipation. Well, perhaps it was time to give the gossipmongers some of their wishes. "When would you like to leave, Roland?"

The outside of his eyes wrinkled a bit as he smiled. Those lines gave her a bit of reassurance. They surely showed that he was a man who liked to be happy. "Now?"

He didn't seem to notice that she still had a full bowl of soup and needed to help gather and wash the dishes, too. "After I finish my soup and clean up, yes?"

"Oh. Of course."

"I imagine I'll be ready within the hour."

"I'll be waiting." When he smiled again before turning away, Gretta caught sight of Joshua looking at her very curiously.

"What are you doing?" Miriam whispered

as soon as Roland was out of earshot. "The way you were smiling at Roland caught everyone's notice! You're tempting fate, I think."

"I most certainly am not. I'm doing my best to follow the Lord's advice."

"Which is?"

"He's obviously put Roland in my path for a reason. I need to see what that reason is."

"Maybe he put Roland there to remind you of just how wonderful Joshua Graber is."

"Joshua is wonderful-*gut*," Gretta agreed. "But I don't know if he's wonderful-*gut* for me."

"Roland only wants something Joshua had."

Miriam's words hurt her feelings, even if they might be true. But Gretta vowed to not let her hurt show. She knew Miriam had not meant the statement in a harsh way. "I best finish my soup now. I'll need to help with the clean up, too."

Miriam rolled her eyes. "And we canna forget that Roland is waiting. Waiting and watching you."

At the moment, Gretta knew he was only one of many.

After giving up any hope of eating her

soup, Gretta stood up and looked for her mother. Finally she found her near a back table, eating snickerdoodles and visiting with a trio of her lady friends.

After greeting the ladies, she bent toward her mother. "Roland is going to take me home today."

"Not Joshua?"

"No." Sneaking a peek at the other women, who weren't even trying to look like they weren't eavesdropping, Gretta lowered her voice. "I'll explain things to you and Daed later."

"But Gretta —"

"It's done, Mamm."

When her mother reached out a hand to halt her progress, one of the other ladies clucked. "Let her go, Deanna. Watching her dilemmas makes me feel young again."

Gretta smiled gratefully, then went on her way.

When Roland's buggy left with Gretta inside of it, Josh pretended to be inspecting his horse's bridle. But in truth, he found if he adjusted his body just so, he could watch the buggy go down the lane for just a little bit longer.

He hoped no one would notice.

Of course, Judith did. She'd just come to

stand beside him, and made no secret of the fact that she was very curious about Gretta's decision — and about her brother's almost nonchalant manner about it. "Want me to talk to her tomorrow? I could see what she's thinking."

"There's no need."

"You sure? You look a bit bothered. And her behavior is curious, for sure," Judith added.

Caleb wandered up to the buggy and added his two cents. "I don't know what she's doing with Roland."

"I do," Joshua replied. "And I don't think her behavior is all that curious, either. I know what she's thinking — she's thinking that maybe there's nothing wrong with a boy being nice to her."

"Weren't you nice?"

Recalling his behavior with her, Joshua shook his head. "Sometimes. Others, not so much."

Caleb frowned. "Don't you still like Gretta?"

"Things have changed between us." Shaking his head, Joshua amended his words. "But I still care for her." But he wasn't sure if that was enough any longer.

Judith looked at him in sympathy. "I saw you speaking with the bishop," she prodded. "What did you talk about?"

"About what you'd expect. I told him that I was ready to be baptized."

"I'm so glad."

"*Jah,* me, too."

"Why did it take you so long anyway?" Judith asked. "You could have gotten baptized as soon as you were done with your *rumspringa.*"

"I don't know. Part of me was just being lazy, I suppose. I was afraid to commit to being an adult. To my responsibilities. But those days are over."

"I'm glad about that. Sometimes I worried that you were going to leave us."

"I never even considered not joining the church. I just had cold feet. And, being the oldest, I felt like Mamm and Daed were rushing me, and I was in no hurry to be rushed."

Looking down the empty road where Roland's buggy went, Judith tilted her head. "Why do you think Gretta is acting the way she is?"

"I'm not sure." However, even as he spoke the words, Joshua felt his cheeks heat. He knew all their problems had started when he'd argued with her that afternoon in his buggy. He had a feeling that now Gretta was attempting to find happiness with someone else.

But he was uncomfortable admitting that.

For a moment, Joshua considered trying to keep his conversation private but he knew it was no use. From the glint in his brother's eyes, Joshua realized Caleb knew that Gretta had been spending time with Roland . . . and not with Josh.

"I think Roland's the one pursuing her," Judith added with a frown. "You know how he's always fancied Gretta."

This was news to him. "I didn't realize that."

"You never noticed Roland always following her around during the singings?"

"No."

Caleb exchanged a knowing look with Judith. "Well, he did. He followed her around last summer, too, when everyone was getting together to play volleyball on Friday nights."

Trying to keep everything in perspective, Joshua said, "They went for a buggy ride. That's all. Don't make more of it than it is."

"That's all for now," Caleb warned. "But we all know how Roland is. He's a fellow who goes after what he wants. And he wants Gretta to be his wife."

"She may not want that, though." Tired of

worrying, and tired of having his brother and sister so involved in his business, Joshua opened the buggy's door. "Let's get in and head on home. Mamm and Daed are going to wonder what kept us."

Caleb and Judith got in obediently enough, but there was enough tension inside to make Joshua realize that each one of them was still thinking about Gretta and Roland.

"I wonder if we'll pass them?" Caleb said.

Oh, he hoped not. Joshua didn't mind having competition. But he sure minded being reminded of all that he'd lost.

And hadn't been able to reclaim.

CHAPTER 13

Roland had little to talk about besides the state of the weather. Gretta tried not to let that bother her too much. Instead, as his pretty gray mare pranced along the snow-covered winding roads and the brisk wind kissed her cheeks, she attempted to look at Roland's ways in the best possible light.

After all, it wasn't his fault that his thoughts were so wearisome to her.

When he pointed out the bank of gray clouds forming on the horizon, Gretta tried to listen carefully to the differences between stratus and cumulus clouds and what that meant to the productivity of agriculture in Ohio. But no matter how hard she tried, she didn't quite understand his meaning.

When he told her how he'd read the *Farmer's Almanac* and had memorized the last eight years' records on snowfall for January, Gretta replied that she was impressed with how much he could learn.

Only when Roland pointed to a flower bed on the side of the road and pondered over what color the blooms might be, did she genuinely smile. Blooming flowers she could relate to, especially since they would signal the coming of spring.

Oh, she so needed spring!

Over the last few weeks, her world had felt frozen in time. Joshua's departure left her feeling bitter cold inside. So cold, she knew she needed to set her mind on new joys instead of focusing on old heartaches.

Firmly she intended to include her social life in that realm, too. Roland was a nice man. He cared about her, and enjoyed her company. She needed to appreciate that. Needed to count her blessings that such a wonderful-*gut* man cared so much to make her happy.

Feeling like she needed to move the conversation on, she said, "Spring is always a time for new beginnings. But January has its beauty, too. Each season has something to appreciate."

"That is a good point you have, Gretta," Roland said. "There is a good to be found in most all things." Nodding a bit, he looked at her with fresh awareness in his eyes. "Because you said that, why, I'm going to try to value this time of year as much as I can. Yes, I'll really do my best to look on the bright side. You know what they say, don'tcha? 'If you can't see the bright side, why ya just need to polish the dull one.' "

In spite of herself, she chuckled. "That's a good sayin'."

"It's good, but it's only something I heard before," he said modestly. "You are the one who's making me think of new ideas. Yes, you, Gretta, are mighty wise."

She felt terribly self-conscious, and more than a bit ashamed. After all, she was still comparing Roland to Joshua, and that wasn't a kind thing to do at all. "I'm not so wise, Roland."

"I think you are, and I'm going to remember every bit of our time together, too. You've given me much to think about. Why, just last night I was wishing the skies wouldn't get so dark so early, but now I'm going to think on it different." He slapped his palm on his thigh. "Why, the extra hours of darkness gives me more time to appreciate what I have."

Because she felt responsible, she played along. "And it gives me another hour of rest at night, for which I am most grateful."

"The snow gives me an excuse to go walking and look for hares." Somewhat shyly he added, "Sometimes I don't go hunting

196

neither. Sometimes I just look for rabbits because I think they're one of the Lord's kindest creatures."

In spite of herself, Gretta felt her heart melt. Roland really was trying so hard to please. He'd known that she had a soft spot for rabbits and didn't want to upset her.

Now, when was the last time Joshua had been so considerate of her feelings? She couldn't remember.

"I like rabbits as well. One time I saw a mother rabbit in spring with two babies. They were sweet."

"Once I held a bunny in my palm."

Hesitantly she added, "And I like to read a fair bit, as well. I enjoy sitting next to our front window and watching the sun come up with a hot cup of coffee."

"Watching the sun rise is surely a wondrous gift." As they plodded along in his buggy, the cold banks of snow passing with each yard, Roland ventured, "I also enjoy prayer in the morning, too."

That's how Roland was, Gretta decided. Careful and contemplative. Full of hope and sunshine. He was a kind man, and a man who was always considerate of others. He would be easy to be married to. A wonderful partner for life.

She could already see that he would be

the type of husband to plan his day around her morning cup of coffee with a book, just so that she would be happy. "I enjoy prayer, too."

"*Sur gut, jah?*"

"Yes."

"Gretta, if we turn right we'll be at your home in no time. Is that what you wish?"

Oh, he was so aware of her needs. So eager to make her happy. Recalling the last time they'd gone skating, when Joshua had acted like their time together was as bad as visiting the dentist for a hurt tooth, Gretta smiled at Roland. "I would like to ride with you a bit more, if you don't mind."

"It would make me happy, Gretta. But the air is crisp, I fear you might get chilled. Do you think you will be warm enough?"

Things were chilly in his courting buggy, but they were covered in quilts and her heart was warm. Roland had made it so. His manner was so pleasant, his companionship so easy, he made her feel toasty and happy. "I'm warm enough, Roland." Smiling his way she added, "Certainly not so cold that I'd be in a hurry to leave. I'd like to stay with you a little bit longer, if you want to know the truth."

Motioning his horse ahead, Roland

smiled. "Then we'll continue a little longer, yes?"

"That would be fine. I mean, that would be mighty nice, indeed."

"Anson told me that the Amish don't work on Sundays," Ty Allen announced the very moment they'd walked in the house on Sunday afternoon. They'd spent the morning at a nearby Congregational church and then went out for pasta and pizza for lunch.

Lilly groaned as she brought in their container of leftovers. She knew where her little brother was going with this announcement.

Ty stuck out his tongue at Lilly before turning angelic back at their mother. "It's true."

"My goodness. I didn't know the Amish didn't do work on Sundays. That's interesting," their mom commented as she put her purse down on the kitchen counter.

"I thought so, too. Anson said none of them work on Sundays, not even his dad. They don't clean or anything," he added.

Though he got on her nerves, Lilly had to smile at her little brother's sense of timing. He obviously had a lot to learn about being subtle. His announcement came just moments after their mom had told Ty that he had to clean his room and finish up his book report before he could play.

"Well, they do have to take care of the animals," she said. "And those probably count as chores."

Ty screwed up his face, then made another pronouncement. "Yeah, but that's it. So . . . I don't want to work on Sundays either."

"Well, the Bible does say we all need a day of rest. You might have a point there." With a wink in Lilly's direction, their mother asked Ty a question. "If you don't plan to do any work today, what do you plan to do?"

"Play with my trucks in the basement."

"Ah. But what about your homework? It's due tomorrow, isn't it?"

"That counts as work, so I don't think I should have to do it." Looking serious, Ty added, "Mommy, you might need to write my teacher about that."

"What about making your bed and putting away your laundry?"

"That's a lot of work, Mom." Tilting his chin a bit, Ty added, "I like having Sundays off."

"But that's not really our way, you know. We do catch up chores and homework on Sunday afternoons."

Chewing on his bottom lip, Ty made

another pronouncement. "Then I might want to become Amish real soon."

After motioning to her mother that she would answer this one, Lilly murmured, "Wow. I think that's really commendable."

His eyes widened. "You do?"

"Yep. I can't wait to see you give up all those toys in your room. And your television shows, too."

"Wait a minute —"

"No television or Hot Wheels, Ty." Tapping her foot, she tried to look like she was thinking hard. "Hmm . . . I wonder where we could donate all your things?"

"Do you think even people who become Amish have to give up that stuff?"

"I do. Joshua said he knows a lady who was once English and she had to give up all her things."

He paused. "I guess I don't need to watch television anymore."

"Then we'll have to get you a horse."

"That would be great! I like Jim."

"Jim's a good horse, that's true. Now, since the rest of us aren't Amish, you're going to have to promise to take good care of him."

"I will. I feed Jim carrots all the time."

"He'll need more than carrots. You'll have to feed him oats and hay in the morning and walk him and clean his stall."

"Anson doesn't do all that," Ty blurted, obviously taken aback.

"I think he does more than you realize. Sometimes he even works at five and six in the morning. Every morning. Even on Saturdays."

"But I can't do all those chores. I have basketball practice at the school."

"You won't if you're Amish."

"I think I'm only going to be Amish on Sundays."

Crossing her arms over her chest, their mother glared. "Sorry, but that is not an option. Since you're not Amish yet, go do your homework."

Lip out, Ty did as he was asked and left the room. Once they were alone, Lilly grinned at her mom. "I had forgotten how hard it used to be to win a battle of words with you."

"Used to be? You mean you don't think I can beat you anymore?"

Looking at her mother, all five-feet-four inches of her, Lilly felt a warmth cascade through her. Barb Allen was a good woman, and had worked hard all her life to be a good mother. Funny how she was just now recognizing those things. "Some days, I definitely think you can get the best of me."

202

"But on others?"

"Others, I think I could give you a run for your money."

For a long moment, her mom looked like she was going to find fault with that, then her face, too, melted into a wide smile. "I think you're exactly right. On some days, I think you've definitely given me a run for my money." Walking across the kitchen, she sat on a chair across from Lilly. "So, how are you feeling? I know you were a bit morning sick yesterday."

"Oh, I felt queasy. I was so tired, too."

"But today, you're feeling a little better?"

Lilly rocked her hand back and forth. "So-so." Of course, today it wasn't her physical ailments that were bothering her as much as the mental strain she was feeling.

"Things will get better. Before you know it, the tiredness will pass and you'll feel like yourself once again."

"I know."

"And when Ms. Vonn stops by again, we'll definitely know how to plan for the next steps."

Shame flew through her. She needed to tell her parents what she did. How Kelly Vonn wasn't going to stop by anytime soon because she'd canceled all the adoption plans.

But Lilly knew what would happen if she did tell her mom. Things would morph into a huge discussion and tears would follow. Lilly would end up feeling like she was the worst person in the world — and bitterly angry that her parents couldn't recognize her maturity.

Yes, it was on the tip of her tongue to tell her mother that she'd made her decision. In fact, she'd already practiced how she'd explain things. She'd slowly talk about how she really didn't want to give her baby away to anyone. That she wanted to be the baby's mother, for better or worse. It was what felt right in her heart. Even though she knew there were a lot of good people out there who would be good parents, they wouldn't be her.

None of them would be the baby's birth mother.

Only she could be that.

But even though Lilly knew she needed to share all that information, she didn't.

Because right this minute, things were good. For once, things were nice between her and her mom. All of the tension that had permeated every conversation had lifted, leaving just the two of them sitting together, remembering how things used to be.

Remembering how much they still enjoyed each other's company. It had been so absent, and she wasn't in any hurry to call the tension back.

And, well, she did have months of being pregnant to get through. Weeks and weeks to let them know about her decision. Weeks and months to deal with the aftermath of that.

So for now, she knew it was time to do something else besides stew. "I think I'm going to look for a job tomorrow."

"Really? Are you sure you're up for that?"

"I think so. I feel fine, and I can't sit around here any longer. All I do is worry about the future."

"You have more to do than that, silly. You've got all your schoolwork! We have to make sure you get all A's so you can get into college."

"I'll get it done. I need to be around other people, Mom. And, you know how I like to be busy, how I need to be busy. Last year I played volleyball, worked at the pancake house, and still did a lot of things with Alec and my girlfriends."

Looking her over, her mother slowly nodded. "You're right. I'd forgotten how busy you used to be. It seemed like every time I turned around, you were on your way to another event." A smile flashed. "I guess I've gotten used to you being here. Do you have any place in mind?"

"I saw that there was a Help Wanted sign outside the Sugarcreek Inn. I thought I'd go in and check it out."

"Just promise me that you'll listen to your body if you get too tired. You've now got someone else to think about, you know."

"I know." Though her mother probably hadn't meant anything by the reference to the baby, Lilly felt so happy that she'd even mentioned it. Maybe when her mom found out the truth, she wouldn't act like it was the biggest mistake of her life. "I'll be careful," she promised.

On Monday morning, when Lilly was driving into town to fill out an application, she wondered if perhaps things were about to change. Maybe they'd get better. Maybe she'd even meet someone at the restaurant, make a friend.

She was so tired of feeling all alone.

But if she didn't, she vowed right then and there to begin to confide in someone who had always been right beside her, right from the start, her heavenly Father.

She knew in her heart that He'd been with her during the whole experience. Perhaps it was time to start reaching to Him like a friend. To have conversation with the only one who was sure to understand her feelings and to be supportive of her, no matter what.

In the silence of the car, as she reached out to Him, she suddenly realized He'd always been reaching out to her, too. She'd never been as alone as she thought she'd been.

It was a welcome feeling — much like the feeling she'd had when she'd first become a Christian when she was fifteen. Until that time, she'd only gone to church because it was what her family did. But one day in Bible study, as they were reading the book of Matthew, everything had suddenly clicked. One moment she was reading about Jesus's struggles, and the next she was applying his lessons to her own life.

She knew she'd walked astray from those convictions over the last year. She'd been struggling ever since she started her relationship with Alec — and choosing to sleep with him didn't help things.

Then, she'd felt too ashamed about her pregnancy to reach out to God again. After all, how could she call herself a Christian while ignoring so many of His guidelines for how to live out her faith.

But now she realized that He had just been waiting for her to reach out to Him. He didn't expect her to be perfect, or to be free from sin. She only had to admit her transgressions and seek His will.

"Oh, Lord, I've been so silly. Thank you for reminding me that you are still on my side. No matter what."

After parking the car, her mood perked up. There was a spring in her step as she stepped out onto the sidewalk. For the first time in a while, she felt hope.

CHAPTER 14

"Hi. I'm Lilly Allen. I called here earlier and Mrs. Kent said I could fill out an application?"

From the other side of the counter Gretta couldn't help but stop what she was doing and stare. This was *Lilly?* The Lilly Allen who had so intrigued Joshua? Well, now. She was far different in looks than she'd imagined.

Gretta had pictured an English girl looking very fancy and worldly, with lots of paint on her face and revealing tight clothes.

But those imaginings surely didn't match with the girl standing in front of her. Sizing her up, Gretta had to admit that Lilly was a pretty thing, to be sure.

Her short curly blond hair was fetching. Her light brown eyes and smattering of freckles across her nose made her look fun and friendly. She wasn't all stick thin either, like some of the English girls Gretta had seen around town.

Her outfit was fairly simple, too — not all fancy. She wore a pair of brown pants and a loose sweater the color of raspberries.

But still, it didn't matter to her whether Lilly was pretty or not, it was terribly awkward to be meeting her face-to-face. Especially since she wanted to work right here at the Sugarcreek Inn.

At Gretta's continued silence, Lilly swallowed and looked nervously around. "Um, I won't stay very long. And Mrs. Kent said there might be an opening. That it was okay for me to apply. I'm just applying to be a waitress."

Now it was Gretta's turn to feel ill at ease. Here she'd been staring at Lilly Allen like she was a wolf in the hen house. "I'm sorry, my mind went running. Yes, of course, I'll go get you an application. And please, take a seat. I'll bring you some pie and coffee too."

"That's okay. You don't have to —"

"It would be a pleasure. Sit now, I'll be right back."

As Lilly slowly lowered herself to one of the tables by the front window, Gretta turned and quickly ran to the kitchen.

"You all right?" Miriam asked when she rushed in, her face flushed.

"Oh, yes. But I need to get an application. There's an *Englischer* out there looking for a job."

"To waitress?"

"*Ja.*"

Miriam smiled. "I'm glad about that. Ever since Donna moved away things have been a little topsy-turvy." She leaned toward the open area and peeked out. "Where is she? Does she look nice? I can't see her."

"She looks nice enough. That's her, sitting over by the windows," Gretta said over her shoulder as she pulled open the heavy door to the walk-in refrigerator. "I told her I'd bring her some pie."

Miriam took two steps to the side and looked at Lilly. "She'd just about our age. Well, that will be a nice change now, won't it? Donna was a *grossmutter.*"

"I suppose." At the moment, she was missing Donna the grandmother something fierce. Hurriedly, Gretta sliced a thick portion of coconut cream pie and placed it on a plate. "I better go bring this to her."

"You look nervous. And giving a new girl pie? Why are you going to so much trouble?"

Though Miriam would have lent her ear and offered plenty of advice, Gretta knew the time wasn't right to share her grievances. "It's no trouble. We've got plenty of coconut pie. It won't be a hardship to share."

"I suppose." Miriam tilted her head. "Are you sure there's nothing else going on? You seem like you're on pins and needles."

Changing her mind, Gretta decided to share her news after all. "Actually, I am a bit flustered." Lowering her voice, she confided, "The girl applying is Lilly Allen. *Joshua's Lilly.*"

Miriam's eyes went wide. "No wonder you look so worried! Do you want me to bring the coffee and dessert to her?"

"No, I can do it. She seems nice."

"But she is surely not. She's caused Joshua to look around."

"It's not her fault. I'm afraid Joshua did all that on his own. Besides, I just went riding with Roland, so I'm not one to talk." But even as she said the words, she felt herself blushing. There was more going on inside her head than mere good wishes.

Inside of herself, she was jealous, plain and simple. She didn't like that Joshua had a new friend, especially since that new friend was pretty and seemed nice, too.

"Don't you worry, Gretta. I'll go take this to her." Snatching the pie plate from her hands, Miriam sauntered right through the swinging doors dividing the kitchen from the dining room.

Gretta followed, but kept her distance. She couldn't help but smile as Miriam paraded around the room like a bossy hen. Regally, she nodded to a pair of women who'd recently sat down, then walked over and deposited the slice of pie right in front of Lilly. "There you go."

Lilly stared at the dessert in confusion. "Thank you. Um, this looks great. But . . . I came here for an application."

Gretta closed her eyes and quickly asked the Lord to help her. Stepping out from around the counter, she called out, "I'll bring it right out. Coffee, too."

Gretta trotted back into the kitchen and began looking through a pair of cabinets in the front of Mrs. Kent's office. She was so frazzled, she could hardly think straight! As she opened another cabinet and frantically looked inside, Miriam appeared in the doorway. "Mrs. Kent just called. She said she'll be here in ten minutes. She was so pleased that Lilly was here that she asked if I could ask her to stay to be interviewed."

"Oh, my." Gretta's spirits sank. Before she knew it, she'd be working next to Lilly all the time. "She's going to want to have Lilly fill out an application, but for the life of me, I can't find it anywhere."

Miriam winked. "That, I can help you with." As competently as ever, she wiped her hands on a dishcloth and plucked the neatly typed application from a stack on Mrs. Kent's desk. "Here is one. Don't worry, I'll go deliver the application and tell Lilly about Mrs. Kent's interview. She'll be right pleased, I think."

Following Miriam back into the kitchen, Gretta heaved a sigh of relief. "*Danke*. Now I wonder what I should do?"

"Take a deep breath and roll out the pie dough," she said with a grin. "You're going to need all your wits about you from now on."

Gretta felt like she was in such a fog, she knew Miriam was right. At the moment, she'd most likely forget to put her head on straight.

"You've helped me along a time or two. I'll help you today. Don't worry so, Gretta. We'll get through this together. If it's God's will that brought her here to work instead of the many other restaurants in town, we'll deal with that."

Gretta murmured, "*Danke,* Miriam. I've been running scared here. In fact, I'm so muddled I don't know what to do or how to act."

Miriam simply smiled. "Don't worry so

much. You're a kind person — I'm sure you'll get along with most anyone. And this Lilly might surprise us, yes?"

"Yes. I need to think as positively as possible. And pray! I'll take a few moments and say a little prayer."

"I think that's exactly what you should be doing."

As the doors swung shut behind her, Gretta heard Miriam's usual chatty voice both welcome the ladies and introduce herself to Lilly.

In no time, Lilly was chatting with Miriam and smiling. Just like they were friends.

Gretta closed her eyes and reached out for the one who always was looking out for her. *Dear Lord, please be with me today. I know you have a plan for me and for Josh, and for this Lilly Allen, too, I suppose.*

If you wouldn't mind, though . . . could all our plans work together? That would make me so happy, indeed.

Feeling better, she finished rolling dough, then got to work chopping pecans for a batch of pecan sandies. As she methodically crunched up pecans by putting them in a bag and rapping them lightly with a rolling pin, Mrs. Kent came in, said hello, then walked out to greet Lilly.

Miriam stayed in the dining area, though

whether it was to refresh the table of women's coffee or eavesdrop was hard to know.

After a time, Miriam finally returned to the kitchen, an empty plate in her hands and a satisfied expression on her lips. "Well, that's done."

Gretta hurried to her side. "What is?"

"Mrs. Kent hired her right away. Lilly Allen will begin to work with us tomorrow."

Her stomach somersaulted. She'd hoped to have a few days to get used to the idea of working with Lilly at the very least. "That seems mighty sudden."

"Why? We need the help."

"Doesn't Mrs. Kent want to think about things for a bit?"

"No need. You were right, Gretta. I'm ashamed of the terrible things I was thinking. That Lilly Allen is a nice girl, and real easy to get along with, too. What's more, she talks as if she's a hard worker, which we all will appreciate. I like her."

"Oh."

"I know you aren't sure how Joshua feels about her, but that hardly matters, right?"

Gretta wasn't sure what in particular Miriam was referring to. Was she speaking of how things weren't too good between herself and Joshua? Or of how Lilly was English, and therefore not much of a rival anyway?

Or was she merely thinking of only work? One didn't need to be best friends with a person in order to work well by their side.

"I suppose it doesn't matter after all," she said.

She was about to expand upon that when Mrs. Kent came bustling back in.

"Girls, we are destined to have a very busy week. That's what my meeting was about this morning. I met with a representative of a women's group in Toledo. They're going to be touring the area and want to have lunch here on Wednesday."

Miriam's eyes lit up. "How many women?"

"Sixty-five."

"Oh my."

"Oh my, is right." Already calculating everything in her head, she turned to Gretta. "I need you to make four shoofly pies and several batches of dinner rolls."

"I'll start on that now."

"Miriam, I'm going to let you work in the dining area with Lilly. Lilly's done some waitressing before so she should be up to speed in no time. Already I think the two of you will get along just fine."

"I think we will, too," Miriam replied in her usual excited way.

Though Gretta felt that there really wasn't that much to be excited about.

Looking at them both, Mrs. Kent continued. "Now, one more thing. I promised a church group that we'd provide some box lunches for them tomorrow, so we need to prepare those." She pulled out a list. "You two divide up the chores as you see fit. I need to go run to the Grabers' store for supplies, then I'll be right back."

And with that, she rushed out again.

Gretta couldn't help but feel a little stung. She knew why Mrs. Kent had asked her to bake the pies. She was a very good pie baker.

But she also felt that Mrs. Kent also knew she wasn't near so good with the English as Miriam was. She simply wasn't all that chatty and upbeat.

But perhaps she could make herself be more outgoing. People were reaching out to her lately. At least Roland was. It was time to stop hiding behind her shyness and reach out to them, too.

She'd just make sure she did some reaching out to the Lord while she was at it. She had a feeling she was going to need His help as much as possible.

CHAPTER 15

When Joshua drove his buggy home from a long day of work at the store, he spied Lilly waiting for him on the other side of the hedge. After getting Rex, their second buggy horse, settled in his stall, he wandered out to see his new neighbor. "What are you doing out here?"

"Nothing."

"Oh." Well, if she simply wanted to stand around in the cold, he had nothing to say about that.

"I mean, I've been waiting for you to come home."

"Why?"

"I have news. I got a job today."

"Why, that's mighty nice. Where will you be working?"

"At the Sugarcreek Inn."

He almost choked. "The Surgarcreek Inn?" Out of all the places in the town, she'd picked the one spot where Gretta worked? Well, perhaps the girls wouldn't talk too much. Or at least talk about him.

Yes, surely his name wouldn't even be brought up! They most likely had many other things to discuss.

But his hopes were not to be.

Weaving her way through the snaggle of trees and branches, she broke through to his driveway. "I met a friend of yours, by the way."

"Yes?"

Looking at him strangely, she said, "Gretta."

He played dumb. "Gretta who?"

"I don't know her last name, and I don't need to know it now, anyway. Isn't she your Gretta, the Gretta you mentioned on our walk?"

"She's not mine." Not any longer. It didn't help that he'd firmly pushed her away.

"But she's the girl you spoke of, right?"

"Yes. She is."

"Well, she's really pretty. And nice, too. Plus, Mrs. Kent says she can bake like a dream. I tasted a piece of her coconut cream pie today and it was fantastic."

"She does make a good pie."

"And?"

"And, she is all those things. Gretta

Hershberger is a right wonderful girl . . ." Inside, his mind was racing. What had Gretta thought when she met Lilly? What had Lilly thought when she'd realized that Gretta was the one he'd been courting? He could only imagine the things that had come up in their conversation.

Lilly didn't seem to notice that his voice had trailed off. "Anyway, I can't tell you how excited I am to have a job. I've been going crazy, staying home all day and doing my classes online."

"When will you start?"

"Tomorrow. Isn't that something? Nothing like being thrown into the thick of things. Mrs. Kent said that there's some women's group coming to town from Toledo and they're going to need all the help they can get." She patted her pocket. "I might even make some good money in tips."

"I hope you will do well." Josh meant that sincerely. He hoped she liked working at the restaurant and enjoyed Mrs. Kent. However, he also really hoped she and Gretta were so busy that they wouldn't have an extra moment to spare.

"I hope so, too. I mean, I'll do my best."

She still stood there, looking at him expectantly. It suddenly occurred to him that she was lonely. Unlike the day they'd walked to

221

the river, the clouds were out in abundance today, covering up any chance to feel warm rays of sun.

The cloudy day, combined with the bursts of wind, were enough to chase anyone from standing outside. "Lilly, would you like to come into our house for a bit? It's getting too cold out here just to stand and talk, don'tcha think?"

"You wouldn't mind? It's not against the rules or anything?"

"I'm not sure what rules you mean."

"You know . . . Amish rules. My parents said you all have a lot of rules you have to follow."

"Perhaps we do. We have the *Ordnung,* which is the agreed-upon rules of our community."

"The *Ordnung,*" she repeated earnestly, like she was preparing for a test.

He chuckled. "Having company over is not against those rules. But I need to warn you. Being in my house might give you a crying headache. We're a big family of seven children, just to remind you."

"I don't mind a full house at all. Not even a busy three-year-old. I like kids."

"If you like *kinner,* then you'll be happy inside. Come in, yes?"

"Yes. If you don't think anyone would mind."

"If I thought someone would mind, I wouldn't have asked you in."

She chuckled. "I tell you, Joshua, sometimes your directness catches me off guard."

He wasn't sure what to say to that. He didn't know how to speak in the English way, of filling his talk with half-truths and white lies.

Seeking to reassure her, he added, "We've had English guests over before. Why, we used to have the Wilsons over sometimes. My mamm enjoyed Mrs. Wilson's company." Of course, as he said it, he recalled his mother's warnings about becoming too friendly with Lilly. She hadn't looked very convinced about his protestations that he and Lilly were simply friends.

But perhaps as soon as she spent some time with Lilly, she'd understand more about their true relationship. "What do you say?"

"I say it is cold out here. If you think it's okay, I'd love to come over for a visit."

Then, with a shrug of her shoulders, she began to follow him across the field to his house.

Right outside the front door his little sisters Maggie and Carrie were playing Four

Square. The red ball fell to the ground when he and Lilly neared. They scampered toward them like puppies, then skidded to an abrupt stop when he and Lilly came closer.

He performed the introductions as casually as possible. "This is our neighbor Lilly. Remember we talked about her family?"

Seven-year-old Carrie solemnly nodded. "You're English."

Lilly smiled. "Yes, I am."

"Why are you here?"

"No reason. I . . . I just came for a visit."

That answer was accepted readily enough. "Well, then, welcome, Lilly," Carrie said, right as little Maggie pulled on Lilly's sweater and practically screamed, *"Welcome!"*

"Danke," she replied with a smile.

"We're going inside now," he told the girls. "It's too cold for us."

"We're playing tag!"

"I hope you catch each other good and well," he teased with a laugh before holding the door open for Lilly. "Something hot sounds good, don't you think?"

She nodded, then followed his example and took off her coat and hung it on a peg near his. Joshua couldn't help but notice how out of place her fuzzy jacket looked next to his family's dark-colored coats and capes.

Next, he led her into the kitchen where his mother and Anson were working on Anson's math problems.

They looked up in surprise when Lilly entered the room.

Anson recovered first. "Hi, Lilly."

With a grateful smile, Lilly replied. "Hi, Anson. I sure am glad your arm is feeling better. Hello, Mrs. Graber."

Joshua watched his mother get to her feet. "Hello, Lilly Allen. What brings you here?"

"Nothing. I just happened to see Josh outside and we started talking."

His mother crossed her arms over her chest. "Yes?"

"And . . . well . . . I . . ." Lilly's eyes went wide as she turned to him for help.

Joshua knew his cheeks were stained with embarrassment. Never before had he seen his mother behave so rudely. "I asked her over, Mamm."

"Why?"

"No reason. Just to talk."

Once again, she looked Lilly over from head to toe, just as if Lilly had been covered with a contagious rash. She frowned. And to his surprise, didn't say another word.

Lilly took a step back and looked toward

the door.

Joshua put a stop to that. "Please sit down. So, does hot cocoa still sound good? Or would you prefer coffee or tea?"

She shook her head no just as Anson's eyes lit up. "I would! I'd like some hot cocoa."

When Lilly slowly took a chair, his mother stared at their guest a moment longer, then pulled out a pan from one of the many carefully stained oak cabinets. "I will make everyone some hot cocoa."

"That sounds mighty good, Mamm," Joshua said, hoping his mother would take his full meaning to heart. He was thankful for the drink and for her kindness to Lilly. *"Danke."*

"Yes, thank you," Lilly said quietly.

Though it was probably the last thing he wanted to talk about, Joshua said, "Lilly was just telling me that she took a job at the Sugarcreek Inn today. As a waitress."

"But that's where Gretta works," his mother said, just as his sister Judith entered the room and stared at Lilly, too.

When Lilly seemed frozen, Joshua gave her a gentle nudge. "Tell everyone about the job."

"It's . . . it's just a waitressing job," she managed to say. "I've waitressed before so I think I'll be good at it. I like helping people and being busy." Without hardly stopping for breath, she continued on. "I met Gretta, too. She seems real nice."

Slowly, his mother poured some cocoa and sugar into the hot milk in the pan and gently stirred. "So, will you be working at the restaurant a lot? With Gretta?"

"I'm going to try to. I'm hoping to make some money and meet some more people."

After a moment, his mother said, "I imagine it would be terribly hard to meet new people at your age."

"It has been. I'm being homeschooled now, so there's not an easy way of meeting other teens."

Judith entered the conversation. "There's a big high school in town. Why are you going to school at home?"

"Well . . . it's a personal reason," Lilly replied. Joshua noticed her voice had become awfully quiet. "My parents thought it would be better that way."

In no time at all, his mamm poured five mugs of hot chocolate, then carefully added a large homemade marshmallow to the center of each mug.

Anson hopped up out of his chair and helped her carry the mugs over.

After taking a small sip from her mug, his

227

mom examined Lilly again. "So why is it that you are going to school at home? I'm afraid I didn't hear the reason."

Joshua groaned. "She didn't tell us, Mamm."

As strict as a schoolmarm, his mother stared at Lilly. "But is there a reason?"

Lilly sipped her hot drink then slowly put it down in front of her. "Actually. There is."

They all waited. Well, all except for Anson, who was pretty much concentrating on his hot cocoa.

After another few seconds passed, Judith came to the rescue. "It's none of our business, Lilly. You don't have to tell us a thing."

"No, actually, I think it might be good for me to share this. It's been weighing on my mind. See . . . I —" She stopped.

His mother frowned. "Is it because you want to be near Joshua?"

Lilly looked shocked. "Oh, no! Not at all. Josh is a nice friend and all, but being homeschooled and taking the job at the inn has nothing to do with him. It's because . . ." her voice drifted off as her cheeks bloomed. Then, pushing her mug to one side, she lifted her chin. "It's because I'm pregnant."

Stunned silence met her news.

"You're what?" his mother asked.

Lilly's face turned bright red. "I mean,

I'm going to have a baby. In six months."

Anson's mug clattered to the table. His mother's eyebrows shot to her hairline. Judith looked as if she'd turned to stone.

And Joshua felt ill. Lilly was with child? And she'd kept the news from him, even though she'd talked about how nice it was to have a true friend?

She'd kept her secret while he'd told her all about Gretta and his conflicting feelings for her?

He now felt ashamed and embarrassed and more than a bit resentful.

Why, oh why had he asked her to come inside?

CHAPTER 16

As Lilly looked from one shocked expression to the next, she felt as if her world was falling apart. What in the world had *possessed* her to blurt that she was pregnant? To a bunch of Amish no less! Now they'd probably really wanted Joshua to have nothing to do with her.

Lilly stood up. The sudden movement caused her chair to scrape the wood floor with a loud screech. Wincing, she looked at Josh, at Mrs. Graber. "Sorry. And, um, I'm so sorry about the news, too. I don't know why I said that."

"You don't?" Mrs. Graber's brows drew downward. "You aren't really expecting?"

Oh, this was getting worse. "Oh, no. I am. I just never intended to tell you all."

"I'd like to know why not," Joshua said grimly.

Before Lilly could figure out what to say to that, Judith came to the rescue. "I think it's fine and good that you told us. We would have found out sooner or later, yes?"

Thoroughly miserable, Lilly nodded. "Yes." Peeking again in Joshua's direction, she inwardly groaned. He was glaring at her in distrust. Like she was an invader in his home.

She supposed she was. Here, they'd invited her into their home, and she'd ruined things by shocking them. Stepping backward, she held up her hands. "Listen, I think I'm just going to go on home now."

"But you haven't finished your hot chocolate," Mrs. Graber said.

"It's okay. I'm sure you don't want me here."

Judith looked at her in confusion. "Why would you ever think that?"

"Because of what I just told you. Because I'm not married."

Judith's cheeks turned rosy but it was Elsa Graber who clucked a bit and smiled. "We might be Amish, but we know how *kinner* are made, Lilly Allen. What you said isn't so shocking."

Joshua took a deep breath. "Yes. Please sit down, Lilly. With you standing there, it feels like you're hovering over us."

Warily, Lilly sat. She supposed there were benefits to sitting and seeing this moment

231

through. If she ran from the room, Lilly knew she'd very likely do just about anything to avoid her neighbors. She might as well finish up the conversation. Tentatively, she sipped her drink. Finding it deliciously hot, she sipped again, the liquid comforting her insides. At the moment, she felt so cold from the raw embarrassment of what she'd just revealed. So cold, and so exposed.

Mrs. Graber watched her and smiled in a tender way. "There, now. Drink up. Milk's always gut for the *bobbli, jah?*"

"Bobbli means baby," Judith said helpfully.

"Oh. Yes . . . milk is good for the baby," she replied slowly. Lilly tried to recall a meal when her parents mentioned something like that. She couldn't. Her entire family struggled to forget her secret. "Mrs. Graber, you seem to be taking my news better than my parents."

"Your parents aren't pleased?"

"Uh, no. Not at all."

"What about your man?" Judith asked. "Is he most pleased?"

"No, he isn't. Actually, he's out of the picture."

"What picture is that?" Josh asked.

His question almost made her smile. Almost. "I meant, uh, he, Alec, didn't want much to do with me once he found out."

Alarm crossed Mrs. Graber's features. "Well, my goodness. Now that sounds terribly harsh."

"It was." Then, thinking that wasn't near the whole story, Lilly amended her words. "He doesn't want the baby, but I can't say I'm all that upset about that. Alec and I . . . well, we're not well suited. I'd love to say I did everything right, but I did many things wrong. I liked a guy who I knew wasn't right for me. And I let myself be talked into something I wasn't ready for."

Judith looked at her compassionately. "You made some mistakes."

"I did. It's hard to explain, but I didn't want to make any more by forcing this boy to pretend to care for me and the baby when he didn't."

"No, you can't force relationships," Josh said, looking lost in thought.

"No, you can't." Then, because it felt so good to just talk about everything that had been going on instead of being lectured, Lilly added, "My parents want me to put the baby up for adoption."

Mrs. Graber blinked. "Ah."

"And will you?" Judith asked.

"I can't decide," she said impulsively, giving away to the usual half-truths that she'd

233

been teasing herself with over the last few weeks. But as the caring feelings of the Grabers circled her heart, Lilly knew she could no longer lie to herself, or to everyone else.

"Actually, what I just said . . . that's not true. I have made up my mind. I don't want to give the baby up. Even though there are plenty of good reasons to do that." Flushing, she added, "I've even called Ms. Vonn, the adoption agency lady, and told her the news. So everything's pretty much settled. I just haven't told my parents."

Judith whistled low. "Oh my. They're going to be mighty surprised."

"They sure are. They're going to be surprised and disappointed that I'm not listening to their advice. See, they have a whole future planned out for me. And college, too. Plus, they're going to be upset that I didn't tell them that I changed my mind right away. That I called up Ms. Vonn without letting them know first. It's a real mess."

She looked Josh's way again, but felt the lump in her throat build when he still seemed shell-shocked. Recalling how he'd spilled his secrets to her about Gretta, Lilly knew he was feeling like she'd been less than truthful with him.

Tentatively, she said, "Josh, I really am

sorry I didn't tell you the other day. But being pregnant is a really hard thing to talk about. Especially to you."

"Why me?"

"You're the first friend I've made here, and I didn't want to ruin things. I knew you'd be shocked. I was afraid you'd hate me, and then I'd be all alone again."

"I am surprised, that is true," he said slowly. "But I could never hate you, Lilly. I could never do that."

"I'm glad you don't hate me." Relief and her old friend, guilt, washed over her. When were things going to settle down?

When you start being honest with yourself and other people.

Hearing that voice guiding her — advising her — made Lilly lift her chin. Yes, she'd been slow to accept the Lord's will, but now that she was embracing the truth, she did feel a little bit better.

After studying her carefully, Mrs. Graber patted her on the shoulder. "Well, now we have no secrets, do we? You'll have to come over more often so we can hear how the baby's doing. Please say you will."

"I'd like that, but I assumed you didn't want me and Josh to be friends."

Looking from Lilly to Josh, Elsa Graber nodded. "It is true that I've been worried about my eldest. I didn't like to think of his eyes straying. I wanted to hold him tight to our ways, thinking if I put up boundaries then he would never be tempted to cross them. But that was a mistake, ain't so, Joshua?"

Slowly, he nodded. "I'm old enough to know my mind, and to know my needs. Telling me to not do something that I know is right isn't going to stop me from doing it."

Judith smiled. "Well said, Joshua."

Mrs. Graber continued. "Maybe I, too, have been needin' some learning. Your being here has reminded me about the importance of relationships and friendship, too, Lilly. Nothing's so bad when you have friends to support you. I've been so anxious that I might lose Joshua, that he was gonna stray from everything I believe in that I gave no room for other ideas." She sighed. "To my shame, I even let my worries stray to your family, Lilly Allen. I didn't want to get to know your kin. I didn't want to make friends with your *mamm,* even though she's invited me over for coffee. I do feel bad about that."

"Please don't," Lilly said. "I know my parents have been worried about things between Josh and me, too. They don't trust my judgment anymore. They thought I

236

would never look to a boy simply in friendship."

"And that's all Lilly and me have been, Mamm," Josh said softly. "Just friends. I didn't want to stray from our way of life. I still do not."

"I think I am understanding that now. Now that we're all getting to know one another, I see my mistakes. And I have noticed that there, indeed, is something between the two of you that is strong and solid. But now I see that the something is friendship, yes?"

"Yes," said Lilly. "I'm really thankful for Josh's friendship."

"I think he appreciates you. I'm sorry to say I let my fears close to my heart. I had a mother's worry that your friendship was going to change things. That he would jump the fence and I'd lose him. But I think differently now. I think you need us, Lilly Allen. And once more, I think maybe we need you."

She was shocked. "You might need me?"

"Oh, yes. I need you to remind me about how strong a mother's love is. How it's okay to make mistakes." With a lovely smile she added, "And I do so love babies."

"Now that I've told you all, I wish I'd told my parents the truth, too."

"You should tell them today, yes?"

Lilly stared at Mrs. Graber, touched by the acceptance in the woman's eyes. Oh, if only things with her parents were that easy. "I should tell them, but I'm afraid."

"You should just sit them down and tell them what you're feeling in your heart. They'll understand."

"It's just not that simple. I don't know how to tell them everything I've been thinking," Lilly admitted. "Through all of this, my parents really have been trying to make things better for me. They think by contacting the adoption agency, moving away from our old neighborhood, and keeping everything a secret, they've helped me."

"But it's hard to help when you don't listen, yes?" murmured Mrs. Graber.

"Exactly. Every time I try to talk about my future they start talking about their dreams for me. I hear their words and then feel terrible. Because their dreams are great. I hate to disappoint them."

"Now you will have dreams for your own child," Judith interjected. "You will be a mother with hopes and dreams, too."

"That's true." A sense of wonder filled her as she contemplated the miracle that had been happening inside of her, but she'd been too blind to see. "Those thoughts will be so nice. But maybe they won't all come true either."

Mrs. Graber chuckled. "I can promise you that they won't all come true, Lilly. *Kinner* have a way of growing up and speaking their minds."

"I'm going to do it. I'm going to tell my parents the truth. Tonight."

Nodding in approval, Mrs. Graber said, "Getting things out in the open is the best. Even if at first things are hard."

"Oh, this will be hard. I'm sure of it." Standing up again, she scooted out her chair and picked up her coat. "Well, wish me luck. I'm off to go tell my parents the truth before I lose my nerve."

"Good luck, Lilly," Josh said as he stood up and walked her to the door.

"Yes, good luck," Mrs. Graber said with a smile. "But I have a feeling you won't be needin' any of our good wishes at all. The truth is the best thing. With the truth, everything will work out like it's supposed to."

"I hope you're right," Lilly said before she slipped on her coat. "I certainly hope you're right about this."

When Lilly got home, Charlie was still out, but her parents were sitting in the living room. Her father was on the couch with a paper spread across his lap and her mom was sitting at the bench of their upright piano. Both turned her way when she entered the room.

"Where have you been?" her mom asked.

"Over at the neighbors' house."

"The Grabers? What for?"

"I was waiting for Josh. We talked for a while, then he invited me over and we drank hot chocolate."

Her parents exchanged glances.

"I see," her dad said. "Lilly, I thought you understood our worries about you and that Amish boy. We really don't want you getting too close to him."

Since their words of caution were so much like Mrs. Graber's, Lilly smiled. "It's too late for that warning. We're already close. Really close."

Her mother closed the cover of the piano keys and walked to the couch. "Oh, for heaven's sakes."

Her father picked up the thread. "Lilly, don't you see? You're in no condition to start a new relationship. And even if you were, I think it's a mistake, timing wise. You'll be in college before you know it."

There was that word again. *Condition.* Her irritation at the euphemism gave her all the courage she needed to finally say what was on her mind. "This *condition* is called pregnancy. I'm pregnant, Dad. And, well, I've decided that I'm not going to go to college anytime soon."

"You'll feel differently after you deliver," her mom said. "Once you pick a family for the adoption and have the baby, you'll be thinking about all kinds of new challenges."

"Next year I'll . . . I'll be raising the baby myself," she stated, flushing because she heard herself stutter. Straightening up a bit, she tried to instill some control over herself. "I — I mean I've decided not to give it up."

With a heavy sigh, her dad rubbed his head like she was giving him a headache. "Lilly, we've been through this before."

"No, we haven't. You've told me what to do and think and I agreed with you because I didn't want to make you mad. But . . . I can't do it. I tried to see things your way, but I can't. And once more, I don't think I should have to. I'm keeping the baby."

"Did all this thinking come from Josh? Did he tell you that giving your baby to a deserving home was a sin or something?"

"He didn't tell me anything! He and his mom listened when I told them and said they were glad I'd made my decision and was at peace with it."

"You've already told the Graber family? You told them before you told us?" The injured look in her mother's eyes matched her tone.

"It just came out. I've been meaning to tell you what I decided, but I was too nervous. I knew we'd start arguing."

"Stating our opinions isn't arguing."

"I don't think we need to talk much about it, anyway. I've made my choice and I'm sticking to it."

Her mother's lips pursed. "Well, we'll see how you feel when Ms. Vonn stops by on Friday."

"Actually, she's not coming. I called her a few days ago and told her that I was keeping the baby."

Her mother threw up her hands. "Who else knows this big, monumental decision? The folks at the corner market? All your old friends?"

"Only you and the Grabers and Alec."

"You've already called Alec?" her dad blurted, his voice raising. "What did he say?"

"He pretty much said he didn't care. I don't think he will either. I mean, as long as he doesn't have to pay for the baby."

After a moment's silence, her parents exchanged long glances. "Somehow that doesn't surprise me," her dad said.

Lilly hovered next to the chair across from them. In her dreams, they held out their hands and offered her hugs. In her dreams, they told her that they loved her no matter what. That they understood.

But obviously, those dreams were as much a fantasy as fairy tales.

Both looked mad as could be, and hurt, too. "I'm sorry," she murmured. "I'm sorry I told other people before you. I'm sorry you're disappointed in my decisions."

A bitter laugh escaped her mom. "You're sorry. I can't even talk about this with you right now. You might as well just go to your room or go back over to Josh's house, or do whatever you want since that's what you're doing, anyway."

"You don't want me here?" Lilly felt her bottom lip tremble. She knew they'd argue. She knew her parents would be upset. But she'd never imagined that they wouldn't even want to see her.

"We want you. But I'm in no hurry to talk to you right now." Glaring at Lilly, her mother said, "You know what that's like, don't you?"

Lilly turned away. Behind her, she heard only the strained silence of her parents.

Their disapproval seemed to burn into her back.

And that made her angry. Turning around again, she said, "You know, all these decisions were never about you. It was never about Josh or the Grabers or even about all our friends in Cleveland. It's been about me and what I can live with."

Glaring at them both, she continued. "Whether you two want to believe it or not, in thirteen years, I'm going to have a teenager of my own. I'm going to have to help him or her with all kinds of things. But at least I'll be able to look at my child in the eye and say that I know all about hard decisions and following your heart. Because if I only know one thing — it's that there's no way I'm ever going to be able to look at some kid in the eye and say that I just didn't want to give up my college dreams for him." Glaring at them both, she whispered, "I'm never going to be able to do that."

When she turned back around and started up the stairs to her room, Lilly finally let the tears fall.

Elsa Graber had been right. The truth was all that really mattered. She was hurting and mad and disappointed. But the heavy weight that had plagued her for the last three months was gone.

The truth had set her free.

CHAPTER 17

The restaurant was full and there was a waiting list for tables when Lilly arrived for work the next day.

"I hope you've got your track shoes on," Mrs. Kent teased as she gave Lilly directions. "A bus load of tourists is here for lunch and we need them seated, served, and sent on their way as quickly as possible."

"I'll do my best," Lilly promised, thankful for the full dining room. She needed as much work as possible so she wouldn't think about the previous evening.

After leaving her fuming parents, she'd gotten ready for bed. Then she'd succumbed to a crying jag, which left her body exhausted but her mind full of worries. She'd woken up early, feeling tired and achy.

Now, though, she felt like an Energizer bunny, eager to get as many tasks accomplished as possible. She liked being at work; it was a welcome break from all the drama in her life.

As the tourists ordered chicken soup, looked at maps, and commented on how cute and quaint Sugarcreek was, Lilly took their orders, served them piping hot bowls of soup and plates of pies, then handed them their checks the moment they were finished.

Back and forth she went, fetching coffee, iced tea, hot rolls, and treats. Each time she passed the kitchen, she saw Gretta and Miriam hard at work on pecan pies and batches of peanut butter cookies.

By three o'clock, the tourists were on their way and the regulars had come and gone. Feeling worn out again, Lilly stopped at each empty table to refill sugar containers and wipe down chairs. Wonderful smells emitted from the kitchen made her stomach growl.

And no wonder, Lilly realized with a bit of a surprise. She hadn't eaten a thing since a quick bowl of cereal at eight that morning.

Poking her head into Mrs. Kent's office, she said, "I'm going to take my break now."

"Take an extra ten minutes if you want them, Lilly. You deserve some time off your feet."

"Thanks." She was just about to go search

for a snack in the kitchen when Gretta met her at the door with a hearty slice of blueberry pie and a steaming mug of coffee.

"I thought I'd save you some trouble," she said with a tentative smile. "You like berry pies, don'tcha?"

"I love them. Hey, want to join me?"

"You know what? I just might."

When Gretta returned with a piping hot cinnamon roll and sat down across from her, Lilly said, "Can you believe how busy it was?"

"Oh, I can! The tourists are wonderful-*gut,* but they cause quite a stir. They used to bother Donna so much. She found them to be too noisy and rude."

"I don't mind those folks at all." With a shrug, Lilly added, "They're easy for me to serve. Maybe because I'm pretty much a tourist myself."

"You'll get used to things soon enough, I imagine," Gretta said. "After all, you've made some friends among the Amish."

Lilly knew what Gretta was talking about. Obviously she was worried about her relationship with Josh.

"Listen, I promise, I don't feel anything but friendship for Josh. And even if I did, the last thing in the world I want to have is a boyfriend."

Gretta still looked skeptical. "And why is that?"

Lilly figured she might as well get it out in the open. "Because I'm pregnant."

"Oh my." Eyes wide, Gretta murmured, "But . . . who? I mean, where is the baby's father?"

"His name is Alec, and well, I'm not with him anymore. I thought we were in love, but I guess we weren't."

"So now?"

"Now I'm going to be on my own." Wincing, Lilly said, "And my parents aren't happy about that. Actually, they're really mad at me. Last night they sent me up to my room, like I was ten years old or something."

"Your eyes are red."

"I guess they are. I, cr . . . cried myself to sleep." As she heard her voice crack again, Lilly shook her head in frustration. "You know what? Maybe they were right to send me off to bed. I'm acting like a child, huh?"

Instead of looking at her like she was a scarlet woman, Gretta scurried around the table and hugged her. "No, Lilly. You're acting just fine, I think. Just fine."

Tears came to Lilly's eyes when she felt the other girl's reassuring hug. So far, Gretta was the one person who hadn't peppered her with questions or offered her opinion about what she should do.

After a moment's pause, Lilly hugged her, too. "Thanks for that," she murmured. "Thanks for not saying a thing."

"I haven't been in your situation, but I do know all about arguing parents," Gretta said. "They can be terribly hard. My parents aren't too happy with me at the moment either."

"Why? You're perfect."

"Oh, surely I'm not that! I don't need to be perfect neither. But I have been in a hard way. See, I've been wanting a future for myself. A good future, and I'm not sure what the right choice is."

"I thought you liked Joshua."

"I do. Well, I did. But now there's Roland, too."

"The other day Miriam said he was nice."

Gretta chuckled. "Yes, 'nice' is really the only way to describe Roland. He's a safe person for me, you see. Roland never makes me feel too much."

Lilly understood where she was going. "And if you don't feel too much, you won't get hurt."

Blue eyes widened. "You understand!"

"I do. But since we're sharing so much, I'll tell you another secret. When you protect yourself from everything, you don't get hurt, but you don't get anything else either. No reassurance, no help. No advice. You're just alone."

Gretta looked at her in surprise. "Is that how you've been feeling?"

"Yes. See, we moved to Sugarcreek because my parents wanted to keep the pregnancy a secret. I was going to have the baby, give it up for adoption, then go to college. I messed everything up when I changed my mind."

"Now everyone knows?"

"They're starting to. I seem to be telling everyone I know these days."

"I bet you feel better now."

Lilly looked at her in some shock. "You know what, I think pretty soon I just might. I think when I'm done crying and feeling sorry for myself I might start to realize that what matters is that I can look in the mirror now. I'm happy with my choice. I feel freer."

"I'll feel better when I know what to do about Joshua. Sometimes we argue."

"That's perfectly normal. All couples argue at least a little bit."

"Well, I don't want to be like that. See, my parents, they haven't gotten along too well in years."

"I don't know Josh like you do. But I have

gotten the impression that he's the kind of person who says what he means. He seems to share his feelings with care, but I don't think he's the cold, silent type. Maybe your arguments with him won't be too bad."

Gretta's eyes widened. "I never thought about his silences as anything but a bad thing. Lately, I've been mistaking Roland's ways as better. But it might be far better to know what Joshua is thinking instead of imagining that Roland is never upset."

"That would be easier for me to take," said Lilly. "Plus Josh is so cute."

Gretta's lips twitched. "Lilly Allen! You said you didn't think of him that way."

"I don't want him as a boyfriend, but I'm not blind. He really is handsome."

"I have always admired his looks," Gretta mused.

"Guess what? I have a feeling that Joshua Graber has always liked your looks, too. And your heart and loving nature. In fact, I think he likes a lot of things about you. He's said he admires your steadiness, Gretta."

"I hope so."

"Listen, your hug made my day. If I was Joshua, I'd want to grab hold of a person who could make me feel good and never let her go."

Gretta stared at her new friend. Such fervent words were mildly shocking, but they made her happy, too. Recalling Judith Graber's words, about heat and passion, Gretta supposed she'd feel sad if that was never a part of her life. If she'd given it all up for safety's sake.

At four o'clock, Josh dropped by. Gretta was making a batch of sour cream cookies when the front door opened with a little jingle. Like a deer in the glade, she stared at him, frozen.

"What do I do?" she murmured to Lilly who was making a new pot of coffee.

"Don't worry. I'll take care of this," Lilly volunteered. And before Gretta could say another word about it, Lilly had walked around the counter with the day's pies on a neatly written list. "Hi, Josh."

"Hi." Cheeks flushed, Joshua was all tense. "I'm here to see Gretta."

Gretta gasped. Oh, but Joshua looked so determined!

Beside her, Miriam giggled.

Out in the dining room, Lilly acted cool as a cucumber. "Why don't you go have a seat? I'll go check to see if she's available."

Joshua looked extremely ill at ease when he placed his elbows on the table.

"Do you want to see Josh?" Lilly asked when she entered the kitchen again. "If you don't, I'll go tell him you're too busy."

"I'm not too busy." In spite of her doubts, Gretta was eager to see him, too. She dusted her hands on her apron and walked out to the dining room. She smiled a greeting before pulling out a chair. "Hello, Joshua. It's nice to see you."

"I'm glad you think that. Lately, I haven't known whether to approach you or not."

"I've just been busy," she lied.

"But you have some time now for me?"

If she'd learned anything over the past few weeks, it was to not be too eager. "I've got a little bit," she said offhandedly.

He cleared his throat. "So, how's the kitchen today?"

"The same as yesterday, busy. I made some sweet bread and berry pies, too. And you? Has the store been crowded?"

"Some."

"And your family? How are they?"

"They're fine." He sighed. "Gretta, I keep hoping things will get better between us, but I don't know how to do that."

"It takes two of us, yes?"

They stared at each other for a moment

longer. Gretta found herself admiring his eyes, not because of their depth of color but because of the new faint lines that had formed around them. They'd given him some character, and showed that he wasn't perfect, not like she used to think he was, anyway.

"Yes," he said softly. "It does take two of us. And I'm willing to try, if you are."

This was her time. This was her choice. *Help me, Lord,* she prayed silently. *Help me know what is right.*

As if someone was directing her mouth, she heard herself saying the right words. The words coming from her heart. "I think I am," she murmured.

"That's wonderful, yes?"

"Yes," she said hesitantly. "Just don't push too hard, Joshua."

Pleasure flashed in his eyes before he hid it again. "Have . . . have I told you about what Maggie said when she was helping Daed with the horses?"

"I can only imagine."

"She said that poor old Jim was a right lucky horse, since he was getting new shoes and all."

Oh, but she did love his sweet little sister! She could imagine the scene with Maggie and Mr. Graber so clearly — just as if she'd been there, too. "That Maggie always makes me smile," she said fondly. "Tell me another story about her. What else has she been doing?"

Joshua grinned. "Everything you can imagine. She's been following Carrie around and fussing with her things." He paused. "I don't have another story about Maggie, but I do have news about Toby. He's finally talking and has been repeating everything Caleb says. It's driving Caleb crazy, of course."

Leaning back, Gretta chuckled. She was so happy to be talking about usual things. So happy to have things almost back to normal.

CHAPTER 18

"Lilly, finally, you're home!" her mother said the moment Lilly opened the kitchen door after work.

"Is something wrong?" Automatically, she started looking for Ty. Her mom had the kind of panicked look that only came when someone was seriously hurt. Had her little brother gotten into some kind of accident?

"No, nothing's wrong. It's just that your father and I have been waiting to speak with you." After taking a deep breath, she added, "Come into the living room and speak to us before you go change."

As worry fled, a new emotion surrounded her. Aggravation. They'd been planning her life again.

After serving food all afternoon, all Lilly wanted to do was take a shower and relax. She definitely did not want to have a serious discussion about her future. Her decision had been made, and if her parents weren't happy about it, they were going to have to learn to accept it. On leaden feet, she entered the living room. "Is there any way we can do this tomorrow? I'm really tired."

"What we have to tell you won't take long," her father said. "Please sit down for a few minutes."

When she hesitated, still in no hurry to subject herself to another interrogation, they looked at each other in a pained way. Like their world was about to end. Obviously, something more was on their minds than her recent decision.

Now curious, she sank into a chair. "What do you need to tell me?"

Her mother looked at her father for a long moment. After he nodded, she spoke. "There's no easy way to say this, so I'll be blunt. Lilly, I got pregnant out of wedlock, too."

"What?"

"I got pregnant with Charlie before your dad and I were married. It . . . it was unplanned."

With some shock she remembered their last anniversary. "No, wait a minute. That doesn't make sense at all. You just celebrated your twentieth anniversary and Charlie's just nineteen."

With a shrug, her mom said, "We lied."

"You've been lying to us? All this time?" Lilly felt dizzy. How much grief would have been saved if her parents had unbent enough to share this news with her! All this guilt, and they'd gone through the same thing! They'd acted like they were so perfect, that she was the biggest fool in the world.

It was unbelievable.

"We got married pretty quickly." With another look at her husband, regret floated across her mother's face. "Actually, we were forced to get married *extremely* quickly. My family was very angry."

"I don't think they've ever forgiven me for ruining your mom's future," her dad added with a grimace. "Even after all these years."

Lilly tried to recall the last time her grand-parents had spent any time at their house. She couldn't. Putting it all together she said, "Is that why they never come over for holidays? Because they're still upset with you?"

"I don't know if that's the reason . . . or if it's because we proved them wrong."

"Wrong, how?"

"We've been happy," her mom said. "See, Lilly, being a stay-at-home mom was never what my parents had planned for me. They had pretty high expectations."

"Like what?"

"Your mother was a literary scholar," her dad interjected. "She could have been a college professor. Could have gotten her PhD. Colleges everywhere were recruiting her to study with them."

"But instead you got married and had Charlie."

"Yes. I've never regretted my decision either. Nowadays, women try to do it all. But back then, it wasn't the case. Girls had to choose."

"And you chose motherhood."

"I did. But I have to admit that I didn't always have an easy time of it. There were moments when Charlie was a baby and your dad was in night school, and I was so tired — so tired I didn't think I could stand up straight — that I would have wished to go back in time."

"Why didn't you ever tell us?"

"I didn't want you to make the same decisions I did."

Her dad continued. "And we never wanted Charlie to ever feel like he was at fault for the choices we made."

"And it's not something I was proud of," her mom added, a faint blush staining her cheeks. "Anyway, we just thought you should see our side of things. Why we've been really wanting you to give up the baby for adoption."

Their side of things. Lilly's mind was running in circles. When she thought of all the tears she'd cried, always because she'd thought she'd shocked her parents, and had disappointed them so much, well, she could hardly think straight now.

Slowly she said, "When you realized that your parents didn't want to forgive you, how did that make you feel?"

With a puzzled frown, her mother replied. "Angry, of course. Sad. And alone. I was an only child, you know."

"I bet you felt like a failure, too."

Reaching out, her mother gripped her hand and nodded.

"Because that's how I've been feeling. I made a really dumb decision, Mom. I knew I didn't love Alec, but I thought I could. And one night, everything just . . . happened."

Her father's lips pursed. Lilly knew she was hurting him. She knew he didn't want to hear the things she was saying. But now she knew that the truth was better than lie after lie. "I didn't want to get pregnant. And I sure don't want to marry Alec."

"On that, we can agree."

"But Mom, Dad, I can't give up this baby.

I know I should. I know I should want to do all kinds of wonderful things with my life without a baby by my side . . . but I can't. That's why I called Alec and Ms. Vonn the other day and told them the news."

"Don't you think you could have involved us in the decision?" her father asked. "You really hurt us when you shut us out."

She knew she had. And she was sorry about it. But she also was a realist. "Actually, I don't think I could have talked to you about it at all. Besides knowing that you would have tried to talk me out of it — I knew it was a decision I needed to make for myself."

"I suppose you did," his mother said after an awkward moment.

"I did." Though they'd probably never believe it, hearing about their struggles had made her feel even stronger. And had made her feel even more comfortable with her decision.

Her parents traded uneasy glances with each other. "We didn't tell you this so you would throw your life away."

"Did getting married and having Charlie mean you threw your life away?"

"Of course not. But things are different now."

"Are they?" Lilly doubted it. Now, more

than ever, she felt as if they weren't treating her as an adult — just a child who had done a stupid thing.

"Very much so. You're not a failure, Lilly. And I promise that you're not alone." Her mother flushed. "Despite what we said last night, we do want to help you."

"Do you? Lately, it sure hasn't felt that way. Now that I know about Charlie, I'm even more surprised by the things you've been saying. Especially since you know about the things I've been going through."

"We do know. But we also know that deciding to keep your baby won't be easy," her mother warned. "You'll lose some of your friends from high school."

"I'll lose the friends who weren't true friends. And if I do, that's okay, anyway. I'm making new friends here."

Her dad's eyes narrowed. "Friends like Joshua Graber?"

"Yes," she replied, daring them to find fault. "Like Josh."

"He's never going to accept a woman who had a baby out of wedlock. Not for marriage."

"I don't want to marry him, Dad. I just want him as my friend."

"You think you two can just be friends?"

"I know we can. Because we already are."

For a moment, the three of them stared in silence, then her father got to his feet. Lilly stood up, too, and within seconds he reached for her. As soon as she stepped closer, he pulled her into the warmest, most comforting of hugs. Reminding Lilly that he still cared. "I love you, Lilly," he murmured. "You won't be disappointed in me any longer?"

"No. I was never disappointed in you, just worried. But no matter what I will always love you."

"And the baby, too?"

To her surprise, his hug tightened as he pressed his lips to the top of her head. "Yes, sweetheart. Yes, Lillian Rose. We will always love you . . . and the baby, too."

The words were such a relief, she started crying. Not sweet, little girl tears, big sobs erupted from her chest.

"It's okay," he murmured, gently patting her back. "It will be okay. I promise."

Lilly closed her eyes and sighed. Finally she felt clean. Of mind and spirit.

And though a baby all her own was growing inside of her, once again she felt part of her family. Part of the family that until very recently, she'd always taken for granted.

Margaret was sitting on Beth's bed again,

being a pest. "Why do you always come in here?" Gretta asked. "You've got a room of your own, you know."

"It's lonely in there."

"And it's better in here?" Gretta knew she sounded sharp, but she was so tired and anxious to be alone. After her busy day at the restaurant, she'd come home to a dozen chores. Each one had felt eternal because of her mother's constant nagging.

"Yes." Lowering her voice, Margaret added, "Besides, you can't hear Mamm and Daed talk in here."

A thin line of dread flew up her spine. She'd had no idea Margaret was bothered by their parents' constant arguments as well. Taking a seat beside her sister, she brushed a long strand of hair off her brow. "What do you mean?"

"My bedroom is right over the sitting room. When Mamm and Daed argue, I hear their words through the vents." Looking pained, she whispered, "It's hard."

"I would imagine it is." Shocked, Gretta turned to her. "Margaret, I didn't realize you've heard them arguing."

"How could I not?" Wrinkling her nose, she added, "I don't think they know I can hear them through the air vents, but I don't know if they'd stop even if they knew I

265

could. Some days nothing seems to matter, you know?"

"I know." Living with their parents was difficult. Some days, Gretta was tempted to count the months until she could leave their home's frosty confines. But to her shame, she'd never considered that her sister was thinking the same thing. For some reason, Margaret's usual happy mood had lulled Gretta into thinking that she was unaware of the constant tension between their parents. "I'm sorry I was so cross. You may come in any time you want. Are they arguing right now?" Gretta couldn't remember if the dinner's conversation had been especially strained.

"Oh, no. I just was feeling lonely. Thinking about when you go get married and I'll be here all by myself."

Dismayed, Gretta felt her cheeks heat with embarrassment. Lately, she'd been only thinking of herself and her problems. "Wherever I am, you can come visit. Always."

"I'm grateful for that, but it won't be the same."

"No, I don't imagine it will," Gretta agreed, curving an arm around her sister. "I'm sorry that one day I'll be leaving you. But I promise I will try and have you over as much as possible."

As Margaret cuddled closer, she pushed aside her long brown hair, hair almost the exact shade as Gretta's. "So, who are you going to marry? Is it Roland now?"

"No one's asked me to marry, Margaret."

"I bet they would if you made a choice. We all thought you were going to want Joshua. Not just Mamm and Daed and me. Everyone I knew thought you were right for each other."

"I thought so, too."

"But now you like Roland?"

Her answer was instantaneous. "No." Gretta felt her pulse jump as she heard herself. "I mean, I like Roland *verra* much, but I don't think he's the one for me."

Margaret scooted away and looked at her directly. "So it's Joshua? He's the one?"

"Maybe."

"You ought to know by now."

"Maybe I should . . . or maybe not. Courting and love are hard things, I'm finding. It's not like putting two seams together on a dress and stitching it up neatly. Sometimes the stitches don't come easy. They knot and get tangled."

Seizing on the metaphor, Margaret smiled with understanding. "Or the pieces don't match up. That's happened to me a time or two."

"Yes," Gretta said, glad her sister understood. "Exactly."

"How are your seams looking now?"

Gretta chuckled. "Like they match pretty good. But, I'm needing pins to hold them in place before they get stitched up."

"What are you going to do?"

"Wait, I suppose."

"Mamm wants you to make a choice, soon."

"Mamm always wants something, and always the quicker the better. Well, this time, she's going to have to be patient. This is something our mother can't force, no matter how much she pushes or complains. I'm not on her time, I'm on my own."

"And Joshua's."

With a smile, Gretta nodded. "Yes. It depends on Joshua, too. That means I'm going to need to wait a bit. Until he is ready and until I am ready, too."

Margaret sighed. "Oh, Gretta, you're thinking too much! At this rate, I'll be married before you."

"Sometimes, sister, I fear that you are right." As she hugged Margaret tight, Gretta didn't know whether to laugh or to cry.

A moment's peace cradled them both,

then like the rumbling of thunder, they both heard their parents' loud voices echoing through the halls.

Margaret frowned. "I wonder why they're upset tonight?"

"Sometimes I doubt if even they know," Gretta said before thinking.

When Margaret looked at her in alarm, Gretta almost took back her words, but then, just as suddenly, she decided against doing that. There was no sense pretending that their parents could get along . . . or that their inability to do so didn't upset her.

Once, Gretta had tried to make their home as peaceful as possible. She'd mistakenly imagined that she could control their anger toward each other. After a little while, she'd begun to realize that there was nothing she could do to make things change. Their parents seemed determined to constantly be at odds.

Then, the front door slammed. Margaret rushed to the window and looked out. "It's Daed," she whispered. "Daed has on his coat and boots and is walking to the barn! Gretta, do you think he's leaving us?"

"I don't know," she replied. She was afraid to lie. Afraid to give false hopes or reassurances.

"What are we going to do if he doesn't

come back?"

Gretta held out her arms and hugged her sister tight. "First, I doubt Daed left us for good. He's probably just walking off his anger or some such."

"But if he does leave us?"

"Then you'll just have to be with me, always."

"Even if you marry?"

Gently rubbing Margaret's back, Gretta nodded. "Yes. Even if I marry, you'll stay with me. If things don't get better, I won't leave you here alone."

"Promise?"

"Promise," Gretta said, closing her eyes.

CHAPTER 19

"How's it coming, Joshua? Do you need help stacking the wood?"

Looking up from his task, he saw his *daed* standing about a hundred yards away, heavy leather work gloves in his hands. Obviously, he was prepared to cross the field and help stack wood if asked.

But Joshua was too old for that. "I don't need help," he called out. "It's almost done." For most of the afternoon, he'd been cutting wood and stacking it into the back of a wagon. Buster, their workhorse, was tied nearby and seemed to be enjoying his time in the field. Buster spent most days either penned in the barn or hitched to a wagon or plow.

Joshua figured he wasn't minding the change in routine either. It was good to be out in the fresh air instead of inside the store.

His father had sent him home after hearing that a fierce ice storm was on the way. Being always a man with an eye out for a dollar, he'd asked him to split enough logs for their home and to sell at the store. If the dire weather reports continued, the store would be busy with customers wanting to stock up on supplies.

Joshua spent the afternoon chopping and thinking and stacking. And though his pile of logs was growing, he still wasn't sure how he was doing with Gretta.

She'd seemed happy enough to see him at the restaurant, he thought as he loaded another stack of wood into the back of the wagon. In fact, when they'd started talking about Maggie and Toby and Caleb, her smiles and comments were just like they'd used to be. Fresh and happy and interested.

But she hadn't quite come out and said that she wasn't interested in Roland Schrock.

With a grunt, Josh hefted the ax from his shoulder, swung down, and neatly split a log in half. Ever since he'd seen her go out for a drive in Roland's buggy, he hadn't been able to squelch the bit of unfamiliar jealousy that had ridden up inside of him.

Now he couldn't stop wondering if her attentions had strayed. Especially since he'd been the one to say he'd needed a break.

How in the world had things gotten so upside down? First he'd been tired of taking things for granted. Then he'd gotten his head turned by an English girl who was no more right for him than a brand new car.

And now Gretta was getting driven around by Roland and he was reduced to calling on her at work. And thinking about their relationship while chopping wood.

He now realized that his harsh treatment of her had bothered her more than he'd ever imagined. Things at her home weren't like they were at his. His parents talked to each other and laughed and argued and then talked some more.

At her house, any disagreement ended in strained silence.

Groaning, he lifted the last of the logs in the back of the wagon, set the ax in there, too, then went to claim Buster.

Buster tossed his head in irritation at being pulled from the little thatch of winter grass he'd discovered under the thin layer of snow.

"I know it's tasty, but we've got no choice," Joshua said as he guided the large horse to the wagon and began hitching him up. "You have to work and so must I."

When the horse blew out air in annoyance, Joshua found himself laughing. "You said it."

He was just about to climb in the seat when he heard his name. "Joshua? Joshua! Wait for me!"

Turning, he saw his brother approach with enough scarves and layers on that he resembled a snowman. As Joshua watched, Anson carefully tromped through the field out to him, nimbly hopping over rocks and a broken tree branch or two.

"Anson, what are you doing?"

"I was playing over with Ty, but I had to come home to do my chores."

"Are they done?"

"Um . . . not yet."

"Daed won't like that. Jim won't either. He depends on you to keep his stall clean."

Anson hung his head. "I know. I was just having a good time, though." Scrambling up on the seat beside him, Anson said, "Ty has all kinds of toys. And his *mamm* made us cookies and we watched cartoons."

Joshua smiled in spite of himself. Before long, these carefree days would be over for Anson. He'd have to accept more responsibility, especially if he and Gretta ever came to an understanding and started building a home of their own. Caleb couldn't take up all the extra chores by himself. "I'm glad you enjoyed yourself, but you need to find pleasure in everything, right?"

Anson wrinkled his nose. "I suppose."

When they reached the side of the barn, Joshua set the wagon's brake, then unhitched the workhorse. Tomorrow would be soon enough to begin carting wood to the store. For now, he probably needed to keep an eye on his brother as he did his chores. "I'm going to go put Buster in the barn. You'd had best get started on the water troughs."

"I will. But first I want to help you with the logs."

"Oh, no. You're not strong enough. I don't think your arm is ready for that, either. Remember, you just got that cast off."

"It's fine. I am, too. I can help you."

Joshua prayed for patience. "I do want your help, but not carrying logs. Go into Buster's stall and get his hay. That will help me the most."

"But I want to stack wood." He puffed his skinny chest out. "Stop telling me no, Joshua."

"I'll tell you 'no' whenever I think I should. Now, go do what I saw. Now." When his brother finally moved away, Joshua directed his attention back to the horse. "Here you go," he said, unfastening the bridle and leads.

He continued to murmur to the horse as he rubbed him down, ready to go inside and rest.

Then, a bit of foreboding hit him hard. Anson should have joined him in the barn by now. "Anson?"

Closing the horse's stall quickly, Joshua hurried outside. He skidded to a stop when he heard Anson's pitiful cries. "Anson?"

"I . . . I'm . . . h-h-here."

He raced to the back of the wagon. And found Anson crying softly on the ground, holding a foot. "Anson, what did you do?"

"I was trying to get the biggest log I could find. To show you how strong I was. But the log was under four others. When I grabbed it, they all rolled onto my foot."

Kneeling down, Joshua tossed aside the trio of logs that covered his foot. Then came up short. "Anson, your foot is bare! Where is your boot?"

"I took it off."

"Why?"

"Mamm just had me clean 'em! I didn't wanna get them dirty."

Praying for patience, Joshua knew it would do no good to point out that the boots were most likely already muddy from Anson's trek across the field.

But in the end, even a quick prayer couldn't stem his impatience. "Honestly, Anson! Do you have no brain in that head?"

"I do! I . . ." Tears came then, overrunning any words that he tried to voice.

Helplessly, Joshua looked at the foot again, just as their father came running from the chicken pens. "What's all the commotion about?"

"About what you'd expect. Anson has been foolhardy again."

"*Daedi!* My foot's all swollen!"

"You're going to be the life of me, child," his father said. "Can you move your foot?"

Anson wiggled a toe. "Not really."

Josh was already sliding an arm under Anson's knees and another around his back. "He's gonna need to go back to Dr. Kiran, I fear."

"You best hitch up Jim, then," their father said wearily. "I'll go tell your mother that it's time to go to the hospital. Again."

"You going to come too, Joshua?"

Joshua didn't miss the hopeful thread in his brother's voice. "I suppose I'd better. Mamm's no match for you by herself. No match at all."

CHAPTER 20

"In case you haven't heard, I'm keeping the baby," Lilly stated to her brothers in the middle of dinner. "I don't want to give it to anyone else. Not even if it would make them happy. I've tried to think about it, and consider giving up the baby. I really have. But I just can't."

Ty stared at her with wide eyes, then suddenly started inspecting his broccoli. Her parents sat in silence.

Charlie, however, looked at everyone directly. "This is news to me. Mom? Dad? You two look almost calm. Have you already heard about this?"

"We have." While her dad didn't look happy with the news, he definitely looked resigned.

Looking at Ty and Charlie, Lilly said, "I know it's going to be difficult, having a baby here, but I couldn't live with myself otherwise."

Ty rolled up a long strand of spaghetti on a fork. "So I'm gonna be an uncle, right?"

Lilly nodded. "Right."

"Hey, you'll be one, too, Charlie," Ty said.

"I guess so." Charlie put his fork down. "Since this baby is going to be common knowledge, I guess we didn't have to move after all, huh?"

Lilly looked at him in surprise. While she hadn't expected him to be especially positive, she hadn't thought that he would still be so resentful. "I guess not. Though, I like it here now."

"I like it, too," Ty said with a smile. "I've made two friends in school, and Anson and me get along great." Since he was sitting next to her, she reached over and ruffled the wayward curls on his head. She could always count on Ty to be on her side.

"So, how do you plan to support yourself, Lilly? To support the baby?"

Lilly couldn't get a sense about her father. Was he mad at her? Trying to scare her? Or, did he think she genuinely needed to worry about these things? "I imagine I'll keep working. And . . . maybe I could live here a while longer."

"You don't plan to go to college?"

"No. Not right now."

Both parents looked disappointed. She

279

knew they were. But Lilly knew that the time had come to stop always being the child. Soon, she would need to be the parent and take on that role.

And that meant that she sometimes had to do the right thing for her and her baby. Not just strive to please her parents.

After giving her dad a look, her mom stood up and left the table.

Lilly still sat, her heart sinking. She'd been a fool to think she could finally tell everyone her decision and expect her parents to embrace that decision with open arms. Obviously there was no chance of anything like that happening.

"Are you going to tell Alec, Lilly?" Charlie asked.

She turned to him, half expecting he, too, to be eyeing her with extreme disappointment. "I already told him. He was fine with it."

Stung, she stared at her plate as her father, too, stood up and left. Moments later, Ty scampered off. Leaving just her and Charlie and a tableful of spaghetti dishes.

"Well, you sure cleared the table, huh?" Charlie quipped.

"Yeah." Lilly shook her head in disgust. "All along, everyone's been telling me to do what I think is best, what's in my heart.

Now that I've done that, nothing's any better. In fact, it's worse."

"Are you okay? I mean, physically?"

"I guess." Actually, she felt sick. She felt sick and awkward and completely like a fool. Maybe she'd just made the biggest mistake of her life. Maybe she should go find her parents and tell them that she was wrong. That of course she was going to pick a family.

Standing up, she gathered three pasta bowls and a salad plate and carried it to the kitchen. To her surprise, Charlie picked up a couple of plates and brought them in, too.

"I think you made the right decision," Charlie said as he started running the water.

She looked at him in surprise. To her amazement, he was staring at her with a new respect and the corners of his mouth tipped upward slightly. Just enough to let her know that he was impressed. "You do?"

"Yeah." Efficiently, he opened the cabinet under the sink, pulled out some dish soap, and squirted a quarter's worth into the running water. Instantly, foamy white suds formed. "What you're doing, it's hard. But you're doing it for the kid. That's a good thing, you know?"

Lilly pondered that as she walked back to the dining room table and picked up more dishes. "I didn't expect you to say that," she said as he took them from her. "I've always thought you hated me for what happened with Alec."

He shrugged. "I'm not going to lie. I sure do wish you'd never gotten involved with Alec. And, I wish you hadn't slept with him." He frowned as he rinsed off a plate and stuck it in the dish rack. "And the baby wasn't good news either."

She couldn't help but smile. Her brother was right. All those things had been rude awakenings and tough to deal with. "But?"

"But . . . things happen, you know?" Dipping his hands into the sudsy water, Charlie swished a dishcloth around, then rinsed and stacked it. "I don't think you're the first girl to fall for the wrong guy and have to live with the consequences. You probably won't be the last."

"So . . ."

Finally, his almost smile turned into a grin. The type of smile that was vintage Charlie. It was a smile that had been absent for a long time. "So, I'm glad you're not trying to pretend that you're not pregnant. That was getting old."

"It was getting old for me, too." She pulled at her khaki pant's waistband. "I'm tired of everyone just thinking that I'm chubby. But most of all, I'm tired of pretending to be something I'm not."

"It's too bad about college, though. Maybe one day you can go."

As they continued the routine of washing, rinsing, and stacking dishes, Lilly said, "I bet I'll go one day. But right now I think it's the least of my worries. Anyway, to tell you the truth, I don't know if I would've been ready to go in the fall. School was never easy like it's been for you. And, well, I like my job at the restaurant. People are nice there."

"Mom and Dad will come around soon."

"I know."

"Don't give up on them. They're just worried about you."

"I hope that's it." Thinking about lawyer bills and baby bills, she shivered. "I never dreamed they'd push me out on my own."

"I don't think they will. Don't worry."

"I'll try not to."

"Lilly, you're going to be fine. See, you've always been so comfortable with who you are, with want you want. Who knows? You might even stay out here in Sugarcreek forever."

She laughed because he made it sound like the ends of the earth. "Thanks, Charlie. And thanks for the help with the dishes. I'll finish up the rest of them now."

He winked, then turned and walked down to his room in the basement.

Of course he hadn't argued with the offer, but she was so glad he'd stayed and talked to her that she didn't even care. She liked the idea that her big brother had decided to support her because he felt it was important, not because their parents had pushed him that way.

As she walked back to the dining room and picked up the last of the serving platters, Lilly reflected on how true Mrs. Graber's advice had been. Truth and honesty always was the best. Even if it meant people didn't hear what they wanted to hear. Even if it was painful.

At least it was out there and honest. And, well, some good had come out of all this, after all. She had the support of some of the most surprising people. Josh, Lilly. Now even her brother had come around.

"Oh, Gretta!" Margaret sang out as she scrambled down the stairs to the basement. "Roland's come calling. Again."

The news created a bit of stir inside her. Fumbling with the dress she was pinning to the clothesline, Gretta attempted to appear calm and collected. However, her voice had a definite squeak when she turned to her sister. "He's here?"

"Oh, yes." Margaret flashed a toothy grin. "Roland is upstairs talking to Mamm."

"How did he seem?"

"Like he'd rather be talking with you, I'll tell you that!"

Gretta grabbed the last of the shirts from the wash bin. After hastily shaking them out, she pinned them on the makeshift clothesline. "Please tell Roland I'll be right there."

Margaret giggled but did as Gretta asked.

After smoothing back her hair under her prayer *kapp,* Gretta walked upstairs and quickly entered the family's sitting room. But Roland wasn't there.

After a moment's pause, she heard his voice from the kitchen. He was talking and talking, just like he always did. From what she heard, her mother seemed to be enjoying his company immensely. Perhaps there wasn't a great need to be rushing to his side after all.

Gretta made her way to the back of the house. She couldn't help but smile when she spied him, leaning up against a counter while her mamm peeled and sliced potatoes.

When she entered the room, Roland seemed to light up. "Gretta, it is so *gut* to

285

see you!"

"It is nice of you to stop by."

"I had no choice. I wanted to see you and church isn't until next week. It was either pay you a call or wish I was," he explained without a touch of embarrassment.

Her mother beamed. "Isn't that so kind of Roland?"

"It is." When she noticed that he didn't seem in any hurry to leave her mother's side, Gretta stayed put in the doorway, feeling for a moment like she was an intruder.

To Gretta's surprise, her mother pushed a pile of peeled and diced potatoes Roland's way. Without missing a beat, he neatly scooped them up and carried them to a boiling pot on the stove, as if he'd cooked in their kitchen a dozen times before. That made her uncomfortable. "Have you been here long, Roland?"

"Not so much."

"Since I knew you were finishing up the wash, I invited Roland in to sit with me," her mother interjected with a pleased expression. "It's been quite a while since a nice young man kept me company in the kitchen."

Since Joshua had never sat in their kitchen, Gretta knew that to be true. But still, it was discomfiting, seeing Roland there, happily chatting with her mother. Acting like he was starting a new habit.

Obviously her mother's viewpoint on Roland had changed quite a bit. She looked now like she would dance and sing if Gretta and Roland decided to court.

But now that she realized no one other than Joshua could ever take a place in her heart, Gretta wasn't quite sure what to do about Roland. "Would you care to walk outside for a bit?"

"I would not . . . unless you really want to walk in the cold."

His reply irritated her. What would he do if she said yes, she did want to be cold? Would he accompany her then? "Oh. Well, perhaps we could go sit in the *sitz-schtupp,* in the living room?"

"That, I will do."

Her mother waved them off. "Yes, you two ought to spend your time together sitting in a cozy room, not out in the cold. Now how about I bring you some snacks and something hot to drink?"

Gretta wasn't sure she even wanted him there that long. His presence felt a bit too pushy. Like he'd taken advantage of her quiet ways. But now she had no choice in the matter — her mother had already made the offer. Dutifully, Gretta said, "Roland, would you care for tea?"

"I would, *danke*."

Happily, her mother pulled out the kettle. "I'll brew a pot and bring it in." With a not-so-subtle wink Roland's way, she added, "I enjoyed our conversation, but I'm guessin' that it's time to have someone else's company for a bit, yes?"

"You guessed right, but I was happy to be with you for a bit, Mrs. Hershberger."

After they sat down and sipped on their tea, Roland began talking. He talked about an upcoming auction for horses. He talked about a recent hunting trip for deer.

He talked about a bunion on his foot and the antics of his eighty-year-old grand-mother.

As Gretta sipped her tea, she watched the clock tick on the wall. And realized that no matter what, she could never be married to Roland. No matter how constant his mood was, no matter how lively his banter could be — Gretta knew she would get terribly ir-ritated with him.

They were not suited.

After almost an hour, he stood up. "It's best I leave now. What time shall I come calling on you tomorrow?"

She noticed he wasn't asking, he was tell-ing her he would come calling. "No. I mean, no, *danke.* Tomorrow's a long workday for me and I fear I won't want much company in the evening."

"You might. A nice chat together might perk up your spirits, yes?"

"I don't think so. Actually, Roland, I think maybe we should cool things off a bit."

"But I thought we were enjoying each other's company. I know I have enjoyed sitting with you and sipping tea."

"I have enjoyed your attentions, but I'm afraid I don't think we will suit each other in the long run."

"We will suit, I think. You just need to give us more of a chance."

"I don't think so."

"But your *mamm* —"

"My mother doesn't speak for me," she said in between clenched teeth.

He blinked. "No. I see she does not. Well, goodbye, Gretta." Looking thoroughly dejected, he put back on his felt hat, and left her house.

Gretta watched from the window as he guided his horse and buggy away from their house and onto the main road.

"I can't believe you just did that," her mother said from behind her. "You tossed him away like yesterday's trash. Honestly, Gretta, every time I think you've come to your senses, you disappoint me again."

Each word hurt. "I'm sorry if I'm disappointing you."

"What are you going to do? If not Joshua, if not Roland, then who will you find to marry you?"

"I'm only nineteen, Mamm. I've got plenty of time to make these decisions. You make it sound like I'm thirty-nine."

"It's only that with Beth gone, your father and I have high expectations for you and Margaret."

"Mamm, I can't replace Beth. I can never be her, or what you wanted her to be."

She looked affronted. "We don't want you to replace Beth. I only want you to think about your future more carefully. Think about what could happen if you make the wrong choice. If you choose the wrong man." Her mother caught herself just in time.

But that stumble finally helped Gretta understand things about her parents. Once, there had been someone else in her mother's life. For some reason, she'd lost that man and had settled on her father. A good man, but a man who she'd always had a cantankerous relationship with.

And so all her hopes and excitement had frozen over time. Beth's death had only made things worse. They'd had no powerful love to overcome the tragedy.

As they stared at each other, Gretta felt sorry for her mother. It had to be difficult to be married to someone who wasn't the love of her life.

But seeing her disappointments only encouraged Gretta to follow her heart. And that person who'd claimed it was still Joshua Graber. Yes, their relationship might not be placid and calm like the still waters in summer. It might be rough and bumpy — but there would be love there. And that love for him would see her through many a difficult situation.

"I'm going to see to the rest of the laundry," she said, though there really wasn't much laundry to see to.

She turned away and went back downstairs. Feeling that her resolve had been uplifted. "Thank you, Father," she murmured. "Thank you for helping me see the light."

CHAPTER 21

Gretta was still contemplating her mother's words the next day when she arrived at work. To her surprise, Lilly Allen was already there.

She had a bucket and a washrag in her hands and was scrubbing the top of each of the tables in earnest.

"You're here early," Gretta said. "Is everything okay?"

"Everything's fine. Mrs. Kent told me I could put in a few extra hours this week if I didn't mind doing a few things like washing tables or cleaning out the bakery case." Still bent over a table, Lilly popped her head up for a moment to meet Gretta's eyes before returning to the spot she was scrubbing. "I told her I wasn't too picky about what I did. I need to save as much money as I can right now."

"For the baby." Gretta immediately felt shamed. Lately, she'd been so wrapped up in her problems that she'd forgotten that Lilly was shouldering a great many burdens of her own.

Straightening up, Lilly rubbed her back and stretched. "Yep. Things are still pretty rocky at home. I want to take on as much of the costs as possible."

"That will be difficult, I think. Babies and children are expensive. Especially for a single mother."

With a little chuckle, Lilly looked at her wryly. "Sometimes you take my breath away, you can be so blunt. But, you're right. It's going to be really hard."

"Maybe your old . . ." *Oh, how did one say it?* "Your boyfriend could help a bit?"

"I don't think he's going to do that. I mean, I don't think he will anymore. By the way, his name was Alec." Smiling again, she said, "I'm sorry, I'm not very good at explaining things, am I? His name still is Alec. I'm just not his girlfriend anymore."

"Does he live back in Cleveland?"

"Yes."

Even though there was much to do, Gretta sat down at one of the tables. "I'm sorry things didn't work out," she said. And to her surprise, she realized that was true. It would be a terribly difficult thing to be facing a future with a baby.

Pulling out a chair, Lilly sat down and faced her. "I'm sorry about it, too. Well, I'm sorry that he wasn't the right person for me," she said. "I'm not sorry he and I are through. Of course, it's not the only thing that I wish hasn't happened." Folding the rag in front of her, she added, "It's been a really crazy time, I have to tell you that.

Gretta felt sorry for Lilly, though a bit of her conscience warred with that pity. In some ways, this Lilly was the picture of every English person some of the more vocal gossips in the community warned youngsters about. She was pregnant and not even attached to the baby's father.

But truthfully, Gretta wasn't too shocked. Even among the Amish some couples married suddenly and had a baby in less than nine months' time. She couldn't pretend that not waiting for marriage vows was only an *Englischer* problem.

Lilly continued. "At first, dealing with everyone's disapproval was really hard. I've always tried to do the right thing, so I wasn't used to people commenting on my actions in a bad way. But then I realized I'd been hoping for Alec to have qualities he was never going to possess — like maturity and compassion." Lilly hopped up out of her chair and started scrubbing tables again.

"Anyway, what's been hard is making decisions that will affect the rest of my life. I haven't known whether to keep the baby myself and raise him or her on my own, or give it up for adoption. It's been scary."

"I would have been scared, too."

"I've been trying to come to terms with how I might feel a year from now. Or two. Or ten." Shaking her head, Lilly soaked the washrag in the bucket, wrung it out, then walked to another table and scrubbed. "I'm sorry. You asked how I was doing and I told you my whole life story. Sorry."

"There's nothing to be sorry about," Gretta said, realizing that she meant every word of what she was saying. "Just because I'm Amish doesn't mean I haven't had my share of difficult times."

Lilly's eyes widened. "I suppose you're right."

"We don't know what the Lord plans for us and sometimes it's terribly hard to guess what the right path is."

"Did you ever make your decision?"

"Yes. But nothing's settled, so old doubts and worries keep returning." She looked at the clock. "I suppose it's time for me to get to work, too."

Lilly's eyes warmed. "You know, Gretta, when we first met, I was sure we'd have nothing in common. But maybe we're not so different as I first thought."

"I'd like us to be friends, if we could," Gretta ventured shyly.

"I'd love that. Thanks, you know, for listening."

"It was no trouble. And you helped me, too. I promise you did. Now I really must get to work or Mrs. Kent will come in to find things not how they should be . . . and our noon customers will be having no cinnamon rolls neither."

"Oh, those cinnamon rolls are heavenly. Save one for me, would you?"

"Of course," Gretta said before leaving the dining room and entering the kitchen. Once there, she found herself smiling. Things did work in peculiar ways, that was for sure. This morning, she'd just made a friend out of someone who she'd at first worried was her enemy.

And in doing so, she learned a bit about herself, too.

CHAPTER 22

Just as everyone who'd visited the store had warned, a large winter storm descended on Sugarcreek and seemed content to visit there for a while.

Over the course of one day, thick fluffy flakes turned to small specks of snow, which turned to pellets of ice and freezing rain, then back to ice again.

The wind picked up and the temperatures dropped.

And still the storm continued. Ice blasted the power lines leading to the building across the street.

From his spot near the window, Josh called out to Caleb, "Go make sure the gas-powered generators are ready to go, will ya? I have a feeling the ice is going to shut everything down. This street might go dark even earlier than anyone's predicting."

For once Caleb looked like he was taking his older brother's words seriously. "I checked them a little bit ago, but I'll go right now to inspect them again. I'll look in on the horses, too. If the weather gets worse, the horses are going to have to stay the night. The icy roads could put them in danger."

"That's a fine idea," Joshua said with some relief. He really needed Caleb's help. For once, it looked like he was going to get it, too.

But there was still something else he needed to take care of. "Listen, I have to leave for a little bit."

"Leave? What are you going to do?"

"I need to run down the street and check on Gretta. I heard she's working today."

"But I bet she's just fine there. There's plenty of work here to do first, don't you think? Surely Gretta can wait."

"I don't think she can," Joshua replied. There was a knot inside of him that couldn't be ignored. Even if they were not destined to be together, she mattered to him. When she was happy, he was. And there was no way he was going to breathe easy if she was sitting alone at the restaurant in the dark. But he wasn't ready to tell Caleb all that — it felt too personal. "Just check on the generators and check the aisles for stray customers. I think most of our last-minute shoppers have left, but you can never be too sure."

"I'll check. But hurry, would you?"

"I'll do my best."

Throwing on his hat, Joshua left through the back of the store and kept his head down as he battled his way down the sidewalk. One hand always needed to stay on top of his head, keeping his hat secure. His other held his coat together.

The short walk up the street seemed terribly long. The wind bit through his cheeks as he took care to watch his footing on the slippery surface.

Around him, only a few cars and trucks were visible. Those that were seemed to be having a difficult time of it, too. They slid and fishtailed through intersections, grinding gears and jerking to stops. Store after store was dark. Signs had been posted on most of the other front doors that they'd closed early because of the bad weather. Even though he'd wanted to stay open late to help anyone who needed a necessity, perhaps he should have done the same thing.

Then he arrived at the Sugarcreek Inn. To his dismay, the sign at the door still read Open and a few lights illuminated the dining area. After trying the handle, he noticed it wasn't locked. Gingerly, he twisted the handle and pulled the door open. "Gretta?" he called out. "Gretta, are ya here?"

He pulled the door open wider. The wind was so strong, it felt as if the door might blow off its hinges.

"Oh! Joshua?"

After turning and forcing the door shut, Joshua faced her.

Gretta was standing near the window, her cloak and black bonnet already on. She looked worried and afraid. But what really took his breath away was the look she gave him. Her eyes went liquid and her whole body sighed. Truthfully, she looked so relieved that Joshua felt like the most powerful man in Sugarcreek.

"Gretta, it's mighty bad weather out today."

"It is." Frowning out the window, she murmured, "The skies are so gray, I don't think it's going to stop anytime soon."

Then she turned to him. "Joshua, whatever are you doing here? Shouldn't you be at the store?"

"I was worried about you. There's no way I could stay in the store without checking up on you. Without making sure that you were safe."

Her chin went up a notch. "That was kind

of you, but I am okay."

"Are you by yourself? Where's everyone else?"

"Miriam never came in today. Lilly didn't either. Mrs. Kent left early to run a few errands, but said she would come back around four or so and get me. My parents can't come — the weather's much too bad to take out a buggy."

He was glad he'd listened to his conscience and had come to check on her. "I'd like you to come to the store with me and Caleb."

"That's not necessary. I'll be fine." Looking out the window she murmured, "I'll just wait for Mrs. Kent to get back."

She was still so unsure around him. Well, he supposed he couldn't blame her. Things had been hot and cold between them during the last few weeks. So much so, that he was never sure how to act around her anymore either.

"I don't know if that will be too easy for Mrs. Kent to do. Everyone says that the roads are bad and that cars are sliding off the road. A few branches have fallen onto the streets, too. The weight of the ice on them is making them break like the smallest of twigs. So the streets are blocked as well."

She bit her lip. "It is worse than I

thought."

"Much worse. Listen, I don't want you to stay here by yourself. I won't be able to focus on my work, worrying after you here all alone. Please, I'd like to take you over to the store."

"How is that better?"

"At least you won't be alone." He wanted to mention that at least they'd be together. And that he could comfort her if she got scared. That he'd make sure she would be fine, no matter what. But he didn't. He was afraid that would spook her. "Will you let me take you?"

She nibbled her bottom lip. "But how will I let Mrs. Kent know that I've left?"

"Why don't I give her a call? She has a cell phone, yes?"

Pure relief filled her expression though her words were far different. "Yes, but . . ."

"Please, Gretta? It will make everything easier."

"You don't have to worry —"

"I can't help but worry about you. Because I care about your safety . . . about you . . ."

"Truly?" Her blue eyes looked translucent, she was staring at him with such hope.

He nodded. "Gretta, I will feel so much happier if you are nearby. And, I'd like to be with you, too."

"All right. I don't want to argue anyway." With a determined expression, Gretta strode to the phone, picked up the receiver, and punched in the numbers. "Mrs. Kent? Yes, this is Gretta. Joshua Graber is here, he's going to walk me to their store to wait out the storm."

Josh watched as she listened intently to whatever her boss was saying. As he watched, it occurred to him that her ability to listen closely was one of the things he admired about her. She was a good listener.

Now he called himself a fool for underestimating her strengths. Gretta was the type of woman who worked well with others and listened to what they had to say. She was able to stand in the background and let others be the center of attention.

Many times, she'd quietly encouraged him but never took any credit for jobs well done.

And he'd taken it for granted.

She hung up. "I guess it's all settled, then." Turning to him, she lightly placed her hand on his arm. "Oh, Joshua, you were right. Mrs. Kent was happy I called. She said in the last hour she'd only gone one mile in her car!"

Still conscious of her touch, Joshua fought to listen to her words. This was the first time in weeks that she'd reached out to him. It

303

was all he could do to not cover her hand with his own. "So . . . she's going to go home?"

"*Jah.* Well, as best she can. Tree limbs are everywhere. She said she'll be glad to know I'm with you, so she can go back home. I just have to lock things up."

Stepping away, she pulled out her ring of keys.

"Do you have any idea of how we can get a hold of your parents? I don't want them to worry."

After thinking a moment, Gretta said, "Perhaps your neighbor friend Mr. Allen could stop by? Lilly said her father passes our home on his way from work."

Thinking quickly, Joshua called the Allen's home. Mrs. Allen was happy to speak to him, but had a nest of worries on her own. Their power was out . . . and the last she'd heard from Charlie was that he was stuck in one of the side streets in town. "When he called, he said he was two blocks from your store, Joshua. I hope he made it."

"He wasn't there when I left, but Caleb is. If he shows up, Caleb will let him in, then I'll ask Charlie to give you a call right away."

"Oh, thank you."

"I'm happy to help. But actually, I called

because I'm needin' a favor myself. I'm taking Gretta over to the store. Is there any way Mr. Allen could stop by and pay her parents a visit and let them know Gretta's safe at the store?" Quickly he told Mrs. Allen Gretta's address. "I think he passes her house on his way home from work. I don't want them to worry."

"You're right, Josh. Scott does drive right past the Hershberger home. I'll call him right now and ask him to stop by and relay the news. Consider it done."

"Mr. Allen's going to visit your folks," Josh murmured to Gretta.

She heaved a sigh of relief. "Oh! Please tell her thank you."

Smiling at the girl next to him, he dutifully said, "Gretta says thank you."

"You tell her that she's very welcome," Mrs. Allen replied. "Now you all be careful, and please don't forget to have Charlie call, would you?"

Now it was Joshua's turn to be reassuring. "I'll have him call you right away. And don't worry about us. We'll all be fine. We've got a generator for heat and lots of food, of course. Would you pass that news onto my folks, too?"

"I'll send Lilly right over. Thank you so much, Joshua."

Joshua hung up. "I, for one, am very grateful for the kindness of friends. Between us all, we'll get everyone informed of our whereabouts."

Smiling, Gretta said, "I'm so glad Mr. Allen will stop by my home. I know my parents would have been very concerned if I hadn't come home."

"It will be all right, Gretta. I don't want you ever to be afraid."

A thread of vulnerability shone in her eyes before she blinked it away. With a smile she said, "You know, most Amish don't care for phones and such, but it's times like these when I thank the good Lord for such inventions."

"I feel the same way."

"We best get going now. Caleb is alone at the store. Others might have joined him by now."

After checking the back doors, Gretta followed Joshua outside. The wind that greeted her blew her skirts around her ankles.

When the lock stuck, Joshua carefully placed his hand over hers and helped to turn the key. Then he held out his hand.

Please take it, he silently offered. *Please take my hand and walk by my side.*

After a moment's hesitation, Gretta slipped her hand in his and stepped close.

Though the temperature was frigid and the wind and ice felt like pinpricks on his skin, Joshua suddenly felt as if he was warmer. He'd missed her. He'd missed this — this feeling of contentment. Of knowing who he should be next to, who he should be walking near.

"Together, it is as if we are both able to fight the weather," Gretta said from his side. "Alone, it was too much."

"Yes."

Gretta was right. Alone, everything had felt too hard and confusing.

Of course, he now realized that he wasn't alone anymore at all. No, to his relief, he felt as if his other hand was firmly contained too.

The good Lord was guiding them to safety. To safety and to each other.

Joshua knew he had never been more grateful.

CHAPTER 23

Charlie opened the door with a broad smile as soon as Josh and Gretta arrived. "Come on in and get warm! Caleb told me I got here not ten minutes after you left, Josh. I hope you don't mind, but I think I'm going to have to stay here for a while."

"I'm glad you're here. I'm sorry I was gone so long. We had some phone calls to make, including one to your mamm," Joshua said as he fought the wind and pushed the door shut with a hearty shove. "Which reminds me, you need to call her up as fast as you can. She's worrying."

Charlie pulled out his cell phone, but his gaze settled on Gretta. "Thanks, Josh. I'll do that."

Catching Charlie's look of interest, Joshua performed the introductions. "Gretta, this here is Charlie."

She smiled sweetly. "Hi."

"Hi, Gretta. It's nice to meet you. Lilly

has said you've been a good friend to her."

"I feel the same way about her. It's nice to meet you, too, though I must say I wouldn't have minded other circumstances."

"You've got that right. Well, I better go call home — *again,*" Charlie said with a shake of his head, then walked a few feet away.

Joshua was just about to offer to hang up Gretta's cloak on a hook when the wind outside gave another powerful whoosh. The gust was so strong, the building shook and windows groaned in protest.

Gretta's eyes searched his. "I fear the storm is getting worse."

"I think you're right," he murmured. Just as he reached for her hand, another blast of wind slammed the building. The lights flickered, then went dark. Outside, the last of the lit buildings turned dark as well, encasing the area in a black shroud. "Well, the power's now out everywhere," Joshua said unnecessarily, just as his brother Caleb approached, holding a lantern.

"It's going to be a long night," Caleb said. "We might as well set up a place to wait out the storm together." He looked around. "How about here? There's plenty of room for us to all sit together but still be able to

309

look outside at the main street."

"That's a good idea," Joshua said. "But first, we have much to do."

Charlie strode forward. "How can I help?"

"Come with me, would you? We'll look at the generator and then take a gander to see what all we might need to make this area comfortable." He turned to Gretta. "Would you take this flashlight and go gather up some blankets and things from the back room? The generator will keep the food in the freezers from spoiling, but the heat won't come back."

She nodded. "I can do that."

Josh smiled at her with a burst of pride. He had chosen wisely. His hoped-for future wife wasn't panicking at all, but pitching in to help in any way she could.

While Charlie and Joshua rushed through the back room, Gretta picked up as many quilts as she could carry and set them on the wide wooden bench near the front desk. She was just wondering what else they might need when she heard knocking at the front door.

There was Cathy Plum, one of her favorite English customers at the restaurant. Gretta hurried to open it. "Mrs. Plum, what are you doing here?"

"For the same reasons as you, I expect," she replied with a frown. "I'm afraid I'm stranded here in town. My stubbornness to heed the weatherman's advice and go right home has gotten the best of me in this storm. Now the streets are too bad for me to drive on. I'm stranded."

"Where's your car?"

"In the back. Joshua and that young man he was with saw me in the parking lot. When I explained my situation, they offered to give me shelter."

"I'm mighty glad you're here."

"I know I'll enjoy your company, Gretta, as long as you dispose of that Mrs. Plum foolishness. Right now, I'm just Cathy, okay?"

"Okay, Cathy."

"Now, what can I do to help you?"

"I just gathered some quilts, but thought I might look to see if there are some blankets we could use, too. Will you help me gather them?"

"I'd be happy to." As the narrow beam of the flashlight illuminated their path, Cathy said, "Who's that teen with Caleb and Joshua? Another stranded motorist?"

"His name is Charlie Allen. He is stranded, but he's also a friend and neighbor of the Grabers."

"Thank goodness Joshua was here," Cathy said with a shiver. "I can't imagine what I would have done if he wasn't."

"He rescued me from the restaurant. I feel the same way." Joshua was proving himself to be a stalwart man. A man to trust during any occasion. He was so responsible, his family left the store in his care. Neighbors like the Allens turned to him for assistance and friendship. Other members of the community were now depending on him for shelter and safety.

Now, she, too, was in his care, and had never felt more cherished. Sometime over the last few weeks, she'd begun to focus on her fears instead of focusing on Joshua's many good qualities.

She'd dwelled on the negatives instead of opening her heart and mind to a bright future. And to the Lord's will.

Now she realized the truth — this time had been a test for her. A test to see what she really wanted. A test to see what she was willing to give . . . and receive. Stopping in front of a stack of horse blankets, Gretta shined her light on them. "Cathy, would you help me gather some of these? They're thick enough to sleep on, I think."

Cathy picked up two as did Gretta. Then they started back toward the front of the store, the flashlight making a wobbly line of light to follow as Gretta carried both it and the blankets in her hands.

As the front windows rattled again, the older lady shivered dramatically. "I guess the Lord really has been watching over me. I'm thankful He gave me this store and your company to weather the storm in."

"I'm thankful for it, too," Gretta murmured.

"Look what we found," Charlie proclaimed as they entered the area, holding a portable stove.

"That looks like something I'd cook with when camping," Cathy said after introducing herself to Charlie.

"That's because this is a camping stove," Joshua said with a grin. "It will let us heat up some water for coffee and such and keep warm."

Gretta pointed to the pile of quilts. "Cathy and I brought these in, and some horse blankets, too. I hope they'll work."

"They'll be great," Joshua said, his voice soft and low.

Once again, Gretta caught herself meeting his gaze and feeling her insides take a tumble. Even though they were stranded in the storm, there was no one with whom she'd rather be. She'd missed him.

As the wind and ice splattered the glass panes in the front door, Mrs. Plum looked at their little group. "Would you all mind too much if we said a little prayer? Though I think He led me here, I'd sure like to think that we still have his ear."

"We'd be most grateful," Gretta said. "Prayer always helps."

One by one, they each bowed their heads.

"The power's out, Mom," Lilly called out from the kitchen.

"Thanks for the update," her mother called down, sarcasm thick in her voice. "I was just changing clothes. Now I'm stuck in the closet, hoping things match in the dark."

Chuckling, Lilly said, "Where are the candles?"

"Candles? Hmm. Some might be in the dining room. Oh, and we might have a flashlight in one of those cabinets on top of the refrigerator. I could have sworn I stashed a couple of boxes up there. Scott? Can you look around?"

"I'll try," he said as he wandered into the dim light of the kitchen.

Lilly looked at him gratefully. "What a mess. I don't know how were going to find anything. We haven't unpacked every box for the dining room and kitchen."

"I'm afraid you're right. I think your mom has put off opening a lot of the boxes since it seemed like we were doing just fine with some of our stuff packed away. I sure didn't think there was any hurry."

"Now we're in a big hurry for candles and flashlights."

"Well, let's see what we can do."

As the wind howled outside, Lilly and her father frantically searched the cabinets for anything that they could use as a light source.

They couldn't find a single thing.

"Boy, this isn't good," her dad said in an extreme bit of understatement. "I don't know what we're going to do if we don't even have any candlelight."

"I'm starting to get a little worried," Lilly admitted.

Slowly, her mom came down the stairs holding Ty's hand. Lilly wasn't sure if she was holding hands to comfort her brother or herself. In the waning light, she looked at them both. "Any luck?"

"None, Barb. We're really up a creek," her dad said worriedly. Lilly noticed that he lowered his voice so Ty wouldn't get worried. "The temperature's going to drop as soon as the sun sets. It's going to be really cold and unpleasant in here in the dark."

"I don't want to be cold," Ty announced.

"I don't either, but we'll be okay," Lilly said, but tried to make her voice sound a whole lot more hopeful than she felt. "Who knows? Maybe the power will come back on soon."

"I doubt that." Her dad patted his cell phone. "I just got a call from my boss. The roads are so treacherous they're asking everyone to stay off of them. Already, there are a number of wrecks outside Mansfield. That's why the phone company hasn't called me in to help man the customer service desks. They're thinking it's just not worth the danger."

"Well, I guess I'm glad after all that Charlie is at the Graber Family Store," her mom said matter-of-factly. "At least there will be plenty of supplies for him and he'll be off the roads."

"He'll be fine," Lilly agreed. "If I know Josh, he's probably rigged up some kind of wood stove and is roasting hot dogs or something. He would be exactly the type of guy to handle any kind of crisis with ease."

Her father groaned. "Don't mention food. I wasn't hungry until I realized that we don't even have a way to open cans. Barb, we really should invest in a manual can opener, at the very least."

"I'll go bring down some blankets," her mom volunteered. "We'll all cuddle in the living room."

"I think we should go next door," Ty blurted, stopping them all in their tracks.

Lilly looked at him in surprise. "That's a great idea, Ty! The Grabers' house will be just fine in a power outage. They don't use electricity anyway."

Her parents looked at each other worriedly. "We can't just show up, Lilly," her dad said. "That wouldn't be right."

"I don't think they'd mind, Dad."

"But we can't even call to see if it's okay."

Ty peered through the frosty glass. "I see lights on in their house. They've got their lanterns going." His tone turned wistful. "I bet they're drinking hot chocolate, too."

Their mom reached out and hugged him tight. "Honey, their house does sound cozy. But still —"

A loud banging interrupted the conversation.

Her father opened the door. "Mr. Graber! Hello! Come in!"

"I came to offer some shelter," Mr. Graber said. "By the look of things, I doubt the weather will clear for at least another twenty-four hours. We'd be happy to have you join us at our house."

Ty scampered to his feet. "Is Anson there?"

"*Jah,* of course," he said with a welcoming grin. "He's there and Judith and Carrie, and the little ones, too. Only Joshua and Caleb aren't home. They're stuck at the store."

"Charlie's there, too," her mom said.

"*Jah.* And Gretta."

Something in Mr. Graber's voice alerted Lilly that maybe he wasn't so worried about Joshua's circumstances. No, he sounded almost bemused that the storm had forced Gretta and Joshua to spend a good length of time in each other's company.

Lilly wasn't worried either. Perhaps this storm was what the two of them needed. A forced time alone to work out their problems.

Her mom smiled. "Frank, I'd love to sit out this storm at your house, if you don't mind. Thank you."

He held up his lantern. "We'll have a time of it, *jah?* But have a care now, it's a long, cold, and icy walk in between our homes."

Within ten minutes, all four of them had small bags packed. Lilly had extra socks, her pajamas and robe and her toothbrush and toothpaste. Then she helped Ty get his things together. He had almost the same

318

amount, except he was bringing a favorite book and some of his Hot Wheels.

Though her parents didn't say too much, she knew they were grateful for the reprieve from the cold house, too. Yet, she also sensed they were a little apprehensive. Lilly had a feeling they were wishing that they'd put in a little more effort into getting to know their Amish neighbors.

It was hard living next to someone and not have much of a relationship.

"Thanks again, Frank," her dad said as they trooped outside and felt a splattering of icy crystals sting their cheeks. "You have really come to the rescue tonight. It's been quite some time since I've seen a coating of ice so thick."

Mr. Graber reached out and tapped a nearby branch with his flashlight. The beam illuminated the thick shiny covering, making it seem like they were in a crystal wonderland. "It's pretty out, but terribly dangerous. Take care with your footing, now."

Slipping an arm around Lilly's shoulders, her dad said, "That's good advice." Leaning a little closer, he whispered, "Are you doing all right, Lilly? Are we walking too fast?"

"I'm okay, Dad."

His hand moved from her shoulders to

gripping her elbow securely. "If you don't mind, I think I'll keep a careful hold on you. We don't want anything to happen to you or the baby."

Though they'd already talked through so much, Lilly's heart warmed as she heard her father's comforting words. "I'm glad you care."

"I do, Lilly. I promise to do better about letting you know how much I do."

As they continued on, one by one slipping through the thick hedge that separated their properties, then slowly climbing the hill that led to the Grabers' home, her father said, "Actually, you've been right about a lot of things. Your mom and I thought we were handling things so well, but in actuality, we were simply living in denial. We thought if we didn't talk about our past — or your pregnancy — if we only thought about your life the way we planned it, it would make everything all better."

"But it didn't."

"It didn't at all. Now we're all going to begin focusing on the present and on the way things are instead of the way they used to be. Who knows? Maybe we'll be all able to count our blessings just a little bit easier this way."

"I hope so, Dad. I've missed how things

used to be."

Holding out his hand, her dad said, "Me too, honey."

Together, they all trooped across the snowy fields, all following Frank Graber's light to his home.

As Lilly held her pillow and small overnight case, she couldn't believe how happy she was — even though the worst ice storm in ages was wreaking havoc on everything they held dear.

Finally, she felt at peace with herself and with her family. Finally, she knew she was going to be okay, even if her future was going to be far different than she ever imagined.

When they arrived at the Grabers' back porch, Mrs. Graber opened the door and shuttled them all in, like a bossy mother goose.

Lilly was pleased to see her parents greeting Mrs. Graber like an old friend and saying hello to Carrie and Maggie, who'd appeared around the corner.

After all their coats and snow boots were removed and lined up against the wall, Mrs. Graber guided them into her large hearth room.

Standing next to Lilly, her mother gasped in pleasure. "Oh, it's so pretty in here!"

Indeed it was. A roaring fire cast a welcome heat to the area. Twin lanterns coated the room in a pretty glow. Two cozy-looking quilts were laid out on the pair of couches, the bright pink and purple squares looking festive and joyful.

Her mother picked up one. "Elsa, this is beautiful," she exclaimed. "The round-the-world pattern is in the shape of a heart."

"*Danke.* I think it turned out nicely, too. I decided to let the spring shine brightly in here for a bit."

In no time at all, Lilly's dad settled next to the fire beside Mr. Graber. Her mom bustled in the kitchen with Mrs. Graber. Judith came in with Toby and sat down on a braided rug.

Ty and Anson were playing with Ty's cars and Anson's wooden farm animals.

Carrie and Maggie arrived with armfuls of dolls.

Things were cozy and happy and felt so homey. So perfect that Lilly hoped they'd get to stay for quite a while.

CHAPTER 24

Cathy Plum got along great with Charlie, Joshua was happy to see. As soon as the stove heated, Charlie brewed coffee with a stovetop percolator and Mrs. Plum took out her knitting and they chatted like they were at a coffee klatch. From what Joshua could gather, Mrs. Plum's son Arthur knew Charlie's cousin in Columbus. They kept saying things like "it's a small world," which Joshua found amusing. Of course everyone was related to each other in some fashion. It was God's way.

Around him, the warm, rich aroma of fresh coffee mingled with the comforting scent of fresh pine. The dim light from the lanterns added a cozy touch, doing much to add to the feeling of security as they waited out the storm.

Caleb was whittling and eating a couple of sugar cookies.

Though there was no need — he'd

checked not an hour before — Josh mentioned that he was going out to check the horses and make sure everything was fastened down well.

After a moment, Gretta said, "May I go with you, Joshua?"

"Of course you can."

When she stepped to his side, her soft gray dress fluttering sweetly around her legs, warm feelings suffused him. For once, they were like they used to be. Before the Allens had come and he'd gotten his head mixed up.

To his surprise, his tongue suddenly felt tied, like he wasn't used to her. Like she was someone new and he was fearful she'd discourage him.

Picking up the lantern, Josh turned to her and smiled. "Ready?"

"Of course."

They walked along the dark back hallway toward the stables. Usually the skylights illuminated the area, but because the storm was upon them, the hall looked black as night. Shadows cast designs along the walls as they walked.

To his right, Gretta shivered.

His first thought was to curve an arm around her shoulders and offer her comfort. Now that he recognized just how much he loved her, Joshua was anxious to protect her in all ways. From storms . . . and from any fears, too. "Are you frightened?" he asked.

"No. Well, a little." She glanced his way, the light of the lantern highlighting the curve of her cheek, the sparkle in her eye. She was beautiful. His stomach twisted with all he could have lost.

"I'm so grateful you came to the store to get me, Joshua."

"I had to," he said simply. "There's no way I could be here if I thought you were in the restaurant all alone. I would have been worried sick."

She smiled at him softly. "I'm fine now. I'm thankful you asked Mr. Allen to stop by my home. I'd hate for my parents to be afraid for my safety."

"I'd never let anything happen to you," he said boldly. Then, at her look of surprise, he felt himself flushing. Since when did he boast so much?

Since she'd become everything to him, he realized.

By his side, Gretta slowed to a stop. She tilted her head up to his. Eyes solemn, she said, "I know that."

His heart thrummed. He swallowed hard, knowing it was time to finally face the future. "Do you think we'll ever be able to go back to the way things used to be?"

Around them, the storm continued to pound. The wind whistled through a few patches in the walls. But as the lantern in his hand flickered between them, Joshua felt as if he and Gretta were the only things that existed.

She flashed a sad smile. "Like how? Like when I thought I was the luckiest girl in the county because you'd taken a liking to me?"

Her words hurt, mainly because he knew he'd deserved it. "I still like you. I always did. I was just worried. I felt trapped, you know. Not just by what we were. But by this store. By my future. By everything." Inwardly, he winced at the pain he saw in her eyes. The pain he knew he'd caused with his indecisions, his confusion.

"And now?"

"Now I feel trapped, but in a different way. I feel as if I'm locked out of the one place where I know I belong." Embarrassed by his words, he stepped in front of her, then turned the handle and led them into the stable.

Immediately, the comforting scents of hay and horses surrounded them. This, he was used to. Horses and hay and stables, he knew how to handle.

Gretta rubbed her arms. "Oh, it's far

colder out here, isn't it?"

"Noisy, too," he agreed. Each ice crystal that hit the walls echoed through the metal, filling the air with a faint buzz. Jim and Buster were standing side by side and looked nervous.

Reaching out, he rubbed his horse's head, right between the ears. "There, now, Jim. It'll be all right, *jah?*" Joshua chuckled when Buster nickered a bit and came closer, eager for reassuring pats and attention. "They're as needy for attention as puppies, aren't they?"

"Indeed." Gretta stepped next to him. When she, too, started petting and talking softly to the horses, Josh looked at her in appreciation. She always did have a way with animals — with anything or anyone in need.

Josh longed to hug her, to hold Gretta close and tell her how much he appreciated everything about her. But he was afraid he'd spook her. Instead, he kept his voice light. "It's good we came out here, don'tcha think?"

"It is." Grinning, she pulled out two carrots. "I hope you don't mind, but I pulled these two from your kitchen cellar. I thought the treats might take the horses' minds off things."

"I don't mind at all." He stood to one side as she gently fed them each a carrot, the horses munching in obvious pleasure.

When the horses settled down some and the winds weren't blowing quite as fierce, Josh took hold of her hand and pulled her closer to the lantern. He wanted to see her face better. He was nervous. He yearned to tell her that he loved her, that he always wanted to be with her.

But was it too late? He hoped to God that Gretta hadn't given up on him . . . that she hadn't looked elsewhere for love and companionship.

"So . . . Gretta, is Roland the one for you?"

Her eyes widened. "I . . . I think not."

Pure relief ran through him. Though every bit of him yearned to pump a fist in the air and cheer, he said, "Why is that?" He needed to be sure Gretta wouldn't have any regrets with her decision.

"Roland, he's . . . calm, but he's too calm. And he doesn't smile or laugh like you do."

"But I thought you wanted someone more calm. Someone who took care to never say anything upsetting."

"I thought I would like that. After growing up in a home where frigid silence ruled, I thought perhaps that I would like a calm husband. A man who I would never worry about disappointing. But the strangest thing happened with Roland, if you want to know the truth."

"What was that?"

"I never knew where I stood with him neither." Eyes shining, she added, "And he was so different from me, Joshua. And so different from you."

"And that's a bad thing?"

"It is. I learned I like many things about you."

He couldn't help it, he laughed.

"I learned something else, too. I learned that it wasn't the words and emotions that were bothering me, it was the way my parents dealt with them. I realized that when they disagree, they'd rather argue and stew than to ever try to make things right."

Joshua felt sorry for her. He always had. He hardly remembered Beth, but he remembered others speaking of her. Beth was outspoken and bright and always cheery. When she'd died of pneumonia, everyone in the community had been devastated.

But most of all, her parents. It was like the life that spurred them on had died with their daughter. And no matter that they still had Gretta and Margaret, it wasn't enough. And most likely would never be.

Gretta had grown up knowing that. Joshua intended to spend the rest of his life showing her just how worthy and special she was.

"So, if not Roland, does this mean I still have a chance?"

"Maybe . . . if it's me who you want," she replied shyly.

"I do." He'd never felt more certain of anything.

She still looked worried. "I'm not just habit?"

"No. I care about you, Gretta. I like your ways. No, I love your quiet ways. I love how you never mind blending into the background, letting other people shine. I love how giving you are. And, I love how, to me, you shine the best. You are a wonderful woman. I . . . I am sorry I never told you that before."

The smile she gave him was so beautiful he stared at her for a long moment, mesmerized by the happiness and, well, sweetness, he saw shining from inside of her. Oh, but he'd been such a fool.

"You don't have anything to apologize for, Joshua. Perhaps we needed this time to understand what we were getting into, you know? Some people need their running around time to sow wild oats. To test the outside world, to test their faith. But we were different, you and I."

He knew exactly what she meant. "We never doubted our faith in the Lord, or our place in the community."

"No, we didn't. But that wasn't enough to make us ready for marriage, was it?" Standing closer, she looked at him with complete trust. Trust that he'd feared he'd never see again. "I think we needed this time to test our faith in each other. To show that we're more than two people following what's been expected of us. We're Gretta and Joshua. Special and unique. And we've chosen to be together."

He liked how that sounded . . . but he needed to add just one thing more. "And we love each other, too. I love you, Gretta."

"Oh!" Tears pooled in her eyes as she gazed back at him. Her hands gripped his as he held them. "I love you too, Joshua."

Opening up his arms, he gently pulled her into a hug and held her close. His heart melted when she curved her arms around him, too, and rested her head on his chest, offering him her trust.

As the horses nickered softly in the background and the harsh wind shook their surroundings, Joshua only wanted to hold Gretta.

He wanted to pretend nothing else existed

but the two of them. Nothing else mattered but their confessions of love and forgiveness.

But Caleb and Charlie and Mrs. Plum were waiting.

After another long moment, Joshua brushed a kiss across her brow, then backed away. "We'd better get on back, don't ya think?" he asked, holding out his hand. "There's no telling what mischief the rest of our group is getting into."

She slipped her hand into his. Hope and love shown in her eyes. "You lead the way, Joshua. Lead the way and I'll follow you. For always. I promise."

Pressing a kiss to her knuckles of the hand he held, Josh picked up the lantern and guided his love back to the store.

Now, forever, they were a couple. As one. Now, forever, she was his.

Nothing could have made him happier.

Nothing could have made him more proud.

EPILOGUE

"It is a happy day, Joshua," Elsa Graber said early on a March morning.

"One of the best," Joshua replied. It was a beautiful spring day, he was surrounded by family and friends, and in just a few hours, he was going to be saying his vows to Gretta.

"Gretta looks like she hung the moon, her smile is so big."

"That makes me happy to hear."

She fussed with his coat, smoothing out a wrinkle that didn't exist. "I have to tell ya, I was nervous about this day. I was thinkin' it might not come. I was worried your head had been turned."

"I knew it hadn't." When she raised her brow, Joshua chuckled. "I mean, it did turn, but not in the way you feared. I was looking out at the world, wondering why the Lord had brought the Allens to live next to us."

"I should think that answer would be obvious. We needed *gut* friends like that.

And they needed us, too."

Looking around at all of his friends and family who had already taken their seats, he spied the Allen family sitting in a back corner. Of course their English way of dress made them stick out like sore thumbs, but other than that Joshua had the feeling that if their clothes and hair was different, they might fit right in.

They were smiling as broadly as everyone else, and looked just as pleased to be there.

His mother followed his gaze, then narrowed her eyes. "Just look at that. There is our Anson, sitting with Ty and looking shifty. He better not get in a bit of trouble today."

"Well, it has been two months since he broke his arm. And a whole three weeks since he sprained his foot."

She visibly shuddered. "Don't even mention such a thing. You'll jinx him, to be sure."

He felt so free, he chuckled. "Perhaps we need to encourage Charlie to take up doctoring. Then we could have someone nearby to help patch up Anson."

His mother brightened. "Oh, but that would be wonderful-*gut!* I'll speak to Charlie about that. But in the meantime, I'm going to go fetch your *bruder* Caleb and remind him not to get his new shirt soiled."

Soon it was time for the wedding service to begin. As always, many prayers were spoken and many passages from the Bible were read aloud. Joshua did his best to listen as closely as he could, though it was hard to look in anyone else's direction besides Gretta's.

The love he saw in her eyes humbled him. Oh, to think he once took such looks for granted! Now he hoped he'd see such sweetness in her expression every day. He silently vowed to do his best to make her happy.

Three hours later, when the service was over and their vows had been said, smiles abounded when they walked out to everyone as husband and wife.

Before they were claimed by all their family and guests, Joshua bent close to her ear. "You made me so happy today, Gretta."

"I'm happy, too. And filled with love for you."

"I love you, too." Right as he was about to kiss her cheek, Joshua was pulled away. Almost everyone from their community had come to share in their good day and were ready to wish them well. Good-naturedly, he caught Gretta's eye. "I'll be back."

"I know," she said with a smile.

■ ■ ■ ■

Five hours had passed and Gretta was thinking she had had enough time away from Joshua. She was eager to start her life with him, by his side. Now she knew that together they could accomplish most anything.

"Gretta? Joshua is looking for you, dear," her mother said.

"Thanks, Mamm. I'll go find him."

"Are you happy?"

"I'm very happy. Thank you for making this day so special for me."

Her mother hugged her tight. "You are so special to me. You know that, yes?"

"I do. I love you too, Mamm."

Wiping a happy tear from her eyes, her mother gestured to where Joshua stood, gazing at Gretta like she was the only woman in the room.

With a feeling of contentment and purpose she had never experienced before, Gretta walked to him.

Dreams had come true and with those dreams came a new light. Gretta realized the light had been shining through all this time. It had simply taken a chink in their daily lives in order to appreciate the brilliance.

Like her dreams, now spring was awakening, bringing with it a new day's hopes and wishes. A new season of opportunities.

And just for a second, just before she reached her husband's side, Gretta held on to the feeling and gave thanks.

Dear Reader,

Thank you so much for picking up *Winter's Awakening!* I hope you enjoyed Joshua and Gretta's story.

I vividly remember the first time I visited Sugarcreek, Ohio. It was in the spring, and the rolling hills, leafy trees, and dark, rich pastures were absolutely beautiful. While there, we visited a number of quaint shops and inns. Some looked distinctly Amish. Others were more Swiss inspired. After eating pie at a local restaurant and visiting a few quilt shops, I knew I couldn't wait to return. Luckily, I have been able to visit several more times — but each visit always feels like it goes by much too fast.

I feel very fortunate that Avon Inspire allowed me to write the Seasons in Sugarcreek series. Each day at my computer, I get to pretend I'm there! I have to admit, it's a great way to spend a day. While the "Sugarcreek" in my book is not an exact match to the actual town, I hope I was able to convey a sense of the beauty and charm of the area.

At the moment, I'm hard at work writing *Spring's Renewal,* Book Two of the series. Already I've fallen in love with my heroine, Clara. I hope you'll like her, too. Of course, Lilly returns. So do Joshua and Gretta and the rest of the Allens and Grabers. Something unexpected happens to all of them, too.

I love receiving e-mails and letters from readers. If you have a moment, please visit my Web site (www.shelleyshepardgray.com) and let me know what you thought about the book! Or, you may write to me at: Shelley Shepard Gray, 10663 Loveland-Madeira Rd., Loveland, OH 45140.

In the meantime, God bless you all.
Shelley

QUESTIONS FOR DISCUSSION

1. Chapter 1 opens with the Graber and Allen kids observing each other and coming to some correct — and some incorrect — conclusions. What has been your experience with first impressions? Are they usually correct? How does a person make a favorable first impression to you?

2. Divorce is almost nonexistent in the Old Order Amish culture. How do you think that influences Amish courting couples? Compare their dating norms to the rest of today's society.

3. Lilly Allen's pregnancy weighs heavily on each member of her family. How could some of their disagreements have been handled better?

4. How do you see Lilly handling the

pregnancy and being a single mother in the future?

5. What do you think about Joshua and Lilly's friendship? Does it seem true to life? Or, do you think it's almost impossible to have a close friendship with a person of the opposite sex?

6. Each main character in the novel experiences an "awakening" — a realization that he or she needs to forge a different path in life. Gretta's awakening revolves around her future with Josh and her own experiences at home. No matter what, she doesn't want to have a marriage similar to her parents' marriage. What are Joshua's and Lilly's "awakenings"?

7. How does the Pennsylvania Dutch saying, "We Grow Old So Fast and Wise So Slow" pertain to *Winter's Awakening*? Which characters could illustrate this saying?

8. The scripture verse from Philippians, "Forgetting the past and looking forward to what lies ahead, I press on to reach the end of the race and receive the heavenly prize for which God is calling us," guided

my writing of the novel. I felt that each character needed to examine his or her relationship with the Lord in order to gain the peace and goals they wanted. Could this verse ever be applied to you, or to someone you love?

9. Have you ever been in the Grabers' situation? Have you ever lost good neighbors and had to learn to get along with far different types of people next door? What were some of the obstacles that you overcame?

10. The next two books in the series will once again focus on these two families. What do you think might be some of the obstacles that the Allens or Grabers will encounter?

ABOUT THE AUTHOR

Shelley Shepard Gray is the beloved author of the Sisters of the Heart series, including *Hidden, Wanted,* and *Forgiven.* Before writing, she was a teacher in both Texas and Colorado. She now writes full time and lives in southern Ohio with her husband and two children. When not writing, Shelley volunteers at church, reads, and enjoys walking her miniature dachshund on her town's scenic bike trail.

The employees of Thorndike Press hope you have enjoyed this Large Print book. All our Thorndike, Wheeler, and Kennebec Large Print titles are designed for easy reading, and all our books are made to last. Other Thorndike Press Large Print books are available at your library, through selected bookstores, or directly from us.

For information about titles, please call:
  (800) 223-1244

or visit our Web site at:
  http://gale.cengage.com/thorndike

To share your comments, please write:
Publisher
Thorndike Press
295 Kennedy Memorial Drive
Waterville, ME 04901